to Dale –
I hope [...] and that I have [...]
convert to medieval
fantasy!

Siera
Torrin

"Rachel Shaw"
12-3-06

THE NECROMANCER'S SCROLL

SIERRA TORRIN

PublishAmerica

Baltimore

First printing

ISBN: 1-59286-294-2
PUBLISHED BY PUBLISHAMERICA BOOK
PUBLISHERS
www.publishamerica.com
Baltimore

Printed in the United States of America

Dedicated to everyone who was begged, bribed, coerced, and pleaded with to read and reread my story.

No humans were harmed in the making of this story. Any resemblance between Roustin and the author is purely coincidental. There is no substance to the rumors that Sevyn is in any way related to the author nor that said author used to use Hunter as a paperweight.

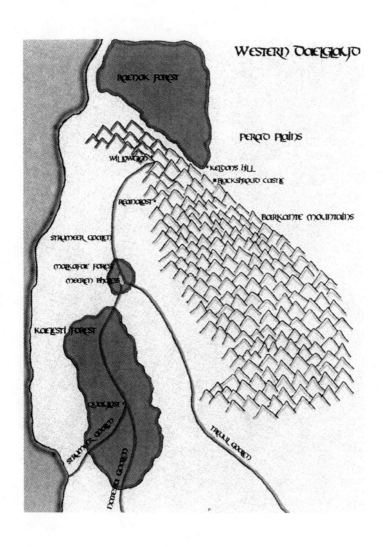

the ancient stables

Kaysie yawned, bored, watching as her best friend rode by inside the aged ring, wearing the old black t-shirt with the silver dragon that Quynn always wore to the stable. The graying fence posts creaked as Kaysie shifted her weight. Her shoulder length brown hair fell into her face, and Kaysie absently tucked it behind an ear. "Heels down, toes up," she said dully to Quynn's backside, as her best friend's horse plodded by in the soft dirt, thinking more about the stones she was throwing that hit the same spot in the old oak by the old wooden stable over and over again.

Her own horse was recovering from a strained ankle and was in the barn munching on hay contentedly. Kaysie could hear the gelding perfectly even though he was in his stall twenty feet away. "Oh, shut up," Quynn said, from the other side of the ring, as she corrected her feet in the stirrups, "Just tell me how I'm doing. Like Carry would."

Carry McLeod had been teaching the girls to ride at Moonstone Stables since they were five. They had always seen her as an old woman losing her mind, though Carry claimed to be only 40. She yelled commands at them during lessons as if they were miles away, or the horse would respond faster if its instructions were screamed. But it was the old tack room that always engaged Kaysie and Quynn's curiosity. No matter how full of saddles and bridles and halters and bottles of fly spray and other horse supplies the newer main tack room got, Carry would never put anything in the old tack room in the back corner of the two rows of stalls. It was rather small, they could tell, and Kaysie always wished she and Quynn could share it.

The horseback riding instructor always forbade it, though they had no idea why.

Kaysie rolled her eyes. I'll give her Carry, Kaysie thought mischievously, taking a deep breath. "GET THAT HORSE CARCASS MOO-VIN'!" she screamed, in her best impression of their instructor, "POSTing TROT! On the RAIL at a TROT!"

Quynn was laughing so hard her horse wandered into the middle of the ring and began contentedly chewing on the tall green grass. Carry chose that moment to come out of the stables. Her straight brown hair lay flat against her back in a long ponytail, held in place with an old black hair band. Bits of hay dotted its smooth surface, giving the impression that she had just fed the horses. Dust rose in beige clouds from Carry's cowboy boots as she came up the dirt path to the old riding ring. "And what's so funny?" She looked mildly annoyed. The girls weren't sure if she had heard them or not. "Fine, you won't answer me? I need two young strong girls to clean out the old tack room. The little one on the other side of the barn. It hasn't been cleaned in the fifteen years I've been here, and your parents won't be here for another couple of hours. Go!" Carry said, making a shooing motion with her right hand.

Sighing, Quynn reigned her horse over to the gate as Kaysie unlatched it. They caught each other's eye, and the look said everything. Did Carry finally want them to clean the old tack room for themselves or was she upset with them? It struck the two as odd, considering the centuries old tack room had been ignored for at least two decades. The only attention it ever received was as the setting of ghost stories. The two put the horse on the crossties in the barn and began methodically removing the bridle and saddle from the horse. Soon, they were grooming the gelding with soft brushes and putting him back in his stall. Quynn pulled back her long straight red hair in an old black scrunchie and began walking toward the old tack room, curious to know if Carry had an ulterior motive for this sudden cleaning. A really bad feeling came over her about the whole situation. "Something's not kosher about this," Quynn said quietly to her best friend, as the walked down the narrow aisle between the stalls.

"Maybe it's a birthday present, " Kaysie teased.

Quynn laughed and playfully pushed her friend. "Come on! You know that's past!"

Kaysie ducked as Quynn tried to push her again and came back up with a large cardboard box. She used it as a shield as they neared the old tack room.

The strong smell of the old leather saddles and bridles were overwhelmed by the smell of mold and dust coming out of the cracks in the boards around the tack room. Most of the stables had been patched over or fixed with new two-by-fours, but the old tack room was ignored, probably because no one wanted to use it. The rumor was that the stable's land was used as a temple for dark gods in old days and that the old tack room was built over the altar for the sacrificed. Kaysie and Quynn thought the tale was laughable, though they loved scaring new arrivals to Moonstone Stables with new and scarier exaggerations to the old legend. Quynn loved the horror stories surrounding the old stables and the grounds. Her quick imagination was a perfect breeding ground for fantastical tales.

Quynn found some old gardening gloves and gave a pair to her best friend. "Happy Birthday," Kaysie couldn't resist saying cheerfully. Quynn pretended to glare at her best friend as Kaysie tugged on the door to the small room.

Quynn loved the smell of leather. There was a leather store at the mall that she loved to go into, just to inhale the aroma of the leather goods. It was a good thing because the smell of leather hit the girls in the face as Kaysie opened the tack room door with a decisive squeak from the rusty hinges. The bottom of the door floated several inches above the floor, as the dirt had eroded over the many decades. Air and dust easily moved in and out of the old wooden room. A visible layer of grime coated everything, making the old room look grayer than it actually was. The girls waved hands in front of their faces, trying to keep the dust from getting in their eyes.

The place was a mess. Old saddles, bridles, halters, lead ropes, and all manner of horse equipment lay scattered around the room. Saddles that had been for old, long-dead horses lay practically glued to the wall with rusted nails. Quynn noticed styles of bridles and saddles from the beginning of the century and wondered how they could have survived. Bottles and tubes and bits of twine made their way into the box, now leaning at a slight angle, propped up by the uneven ground. Moldy hay and palm-sized hairballs that were now gray and brown and covered in dirt and grime were tentatively thrown in the general direction of the box. Every once in awhile, Kaysie and Quynn would pick something completely unrecognizable up with two fingers and ask the other what it could be. After a round of answers that could've resembled a junior high school lunch table full of boys and a lot of giggling, Quynn came across a rather large piece of brown leather, folded several times into a flat rectangle. She stopped, curious, because although she had found many oddly shaped scraps of leather, none had been this big. She motioned for Kaysie to come over to the back corner where she had found the rolled up tanned leather on a saddle stuck to its stand. At first, Quynn thought she had found a big scrap of leather, useful for a leather blanket for one of her sister's dolls. Then, behind her, Kaysie gasped. On the rough side of the leather, the color began to change. It was no longer the rough beige of worn leather, but the tan of aged paper! Kaysie closed the tack room door and placed an old feed bucket in front of the door to keep it from opening. "What is it?" Kaysie whispered.

Quynn had unrolled the leather and looked at the writing on the carefully folded paper on the uneven dirt floor. "It has strange words on it," she finally answered, "And this ain't English."

Kaysie looked over her friend's shoulder as she scanned the paper for herself. The first thing that caught her eye was the intricate ink drawing of a stone tower and balcony. Familiar letters were beautifully scribed flowing around the edges of the tower, but they resembled no words the two girls had ever heard. The edges were frayed and brown, but the words gleamed in the dim light as if they had been penned a few hours previous. Silently, Quynn carefully folded the leather and paper back and hid it inside her hat, and the two continued to clean.

ancient scroll

The girls were brimming with questions. Did Carry know about this? Should they show it to someone? Should they tell their parents? Should they show a museum? Should they keep their mouths shut? Quynn had immediately thought of her other love, her love of all things Medieval. She enjoyed role-playing games, fantasy novels, and the art and history of the time. Could these words be what she thought they might be? Quynn shook her head. I've been reading too much, she thought.

When Carry at last decided the tack room was usable again, she thanked Quynn and Kaysie and told the girls that she would continue cleaning. Soon, their mothers drove up the long dusty road to the stable, and the two girls ran to beg them before either of the women could get out of their respective vehicles to let them spend the night together. Fortunately, it was a Saturday, so it didn't arouse any suspicions. They always begged to sleep over on the weekends.

"Thanks, Mom! You're the best!" Quynn said, giving her mother a tight hug and prompting the older woman to roll her eyes and smile.

"Thank you, Mrs. Dornoch!" Kaysie looked so grateful that Quynn's mother gave her daughter's long time best friend a curious glance, but it ended in an amused smile.

Quynn and Kaysie got out of the old truck and ran to Quynn's room in a flurry of red and brown hair and dirty blue jeans. "You're welcome," came the reply, after a decisive thud of the door slamming shut rang throughout the old farmhouse.

Fantasy novels and thick books on medieval history and art lined

Quynn's bookshelves. Knights and dragons flew on her walls around long State Fair ribbons and trophies won from past horse shows. Detailed wooden horses stood among pewter dragons and painted figurines of elves, dwarves, and human mages. A small teddy bear sat on her bed, the little stars on its black robe glowing faintly in the shade next to another bear wrapped in a white velvet cloak with silver runes stitched all over the cloth. She had painted a castle above her bed, gray stones climbing upwards to the ceiling, flags floating in an imaginary breeze.

The girls practically flew to Quynn's heavy wooden desk and unrolled the leather-bound paper. The symbols and strange words hadn't changed. The intricate ink drawing of a tower along the left side and the stone balcony that seemed to draw the eye towards it still looked as if the ink hadn't quite dried. Other strange symbols were drawn around the paper, with delicate thick and thin strokes making the design and words look like an ancient illumination that the scribe never colored. Kaysie decided to try and pronounce the words. Sometimes things made more sense if you read them aloud, she reasoned. *"'Shieer-ak, tenkits, um, drades kelmond, shehanu, jeras, lefvax.'* No, that made no more sense that it did earlier today. That tower sure is pretty, though. I'd love to be able to draw like that."

"Me, too," said Quynn appreciatively, as she looked at the words over Kaysie's shoulder. Slowly, she mouthed them until she had a good idea on how they were pronounced. Out loud, she tried, *"Shirak tenkets drades kelmund sh'kamu jeeras--"*

A strange tingling sensation waved over Quynn's body, a feeling of power and energy. It felt right, somehow. Suddenly, there was a knock on Quynn's bedroom door. The two started and pushed their treasure under a pile of school papers and sketches just as the door flung open. The feeling passed, like a sudden downpour ending as quickly as it started. It was Carry. She looked as if she had spent more time in the old tack room than Kaysie and Quynn. Her brown hair flew in every direction as if she had been in a windstorm, and

14

dust covered her jeans and old t-shirt, giving the whole ensemble a brown tint. Carry's black boots were looking a bit grayer, though they left no trail from the front door to Quynn's bedroom. The girls tried to look like they were talking about the muscular men displayed in one of Kaysie's teen magazines that was on top of the pile of stuff on Quynn's desk. "What's up? Justin is cuter," Kaysie said, giving Carry a quick wave.

"Hi, Carry. No, Kevin is hotter," Quynn countered.

"Justin."

"Kevin."

"Justin."

"Kevin."

"Did you find anything unusual while you were cleaning?" Carry interrupted, trying to hide the urgency in her voice.

Quynn shrugged. "I think I may have found some new spider species fossilized in the dust," she said helpfully, "And a good science experiment on fuzzy mold and hay."

Carry forced a smile. "Nothing overly important-looking?"

"I didn't throw away any of the saddles or bridles or halters, if that's what you mean. I figured maybe some could be salvageable for a museum or something," Quynn said innocently.

Quynn knew Carry was hiding something. She felt it in her gut. She was pretty sure Carry knew something of the scroll, but for now, Quynn was determined to keep her mouth shut about their find. Kaysie scooted back onto the desk, trying innocently to cover up any leather corners that may have been trying to peak out from under the pile of papers. Carry saw her move out of the corner of her eye, but pretended not to care. "Girls! Dinner's ready!"

Kaysie sighed inwardly. Mrs. Dornoch to the rescue, and she didn't even know it. "I'll see you two tomorrow," Carry said, trying not to sound annoyed.

The next day, the two were scheduled for a long trail ride, a six-mile horseback ride around the stable's forested acres of dirt paths. Early in the morning, the two slid into old riding boots, jeans, and old dark t-shirts, eager to get started, despite the late-night gossip-feast. The scroll had not been mentioned, as if talking about it would make the paper disappear or lose its mystery.

Kaysie packed a small backpack with some snacks, bottled water, and a couple of apples for the horses. Kaysie barely remembered to stuff the scroll into the bottom of the backpack before she ran downstairs to leave. Mrs. Dornoch was leaning on the front door, her right foot barely touching the ground, twirling her keys. Quynn was draped backwards over the arm of the couch, feet hanging loosely in the air, and looking questionably comfortable. Her green eyes were completely shut. "Time to go!" her mom said cheerfully, in the direction of her daughter.

"Unnghh," she said, rolling over on the cushions and burying her head.

Kaysie laughed, grabbed her best friend by the hands, and pulled. Kaysie actually went to the gym to work out, unlike Quynn, who just took along a book. Kaysie's muscles barely strained as Quynn went flying towards the door. "Augh!" she laughed, "I'm coming! I'm coming!"

Mrs. Dornoch only laughed as her daughter whined all the way to the old truck.

Kaysie loved the trip to the stables. The country calmed her. Every turn and twist of the kudzu covered the trees like waves on the sand. Trees that were thick and sturdy with age fawned over each other and over the fencing protecting the trails, as if the fences were keeping the trees upright. Birds floated in and out from between the branches, and deer tugged at small morsels under the foliage. Nestled among the unspoiled nature was the stable. The buildings were rumored to be centuries old. The wooden planks had weathered to a light shade of gray, starkly contrasting with the newer brown-stained additions to the stables. The ground was mostly dirt, and horses and people and barn cats continually trampled the earth. Grass reigned supreme only in the rings and paddock, where although continually attacked by hungry horses, it continued to grow long and thick and green.

The air was warm, and the leaves gracefully floated on the branches and through the summer breeze. Kaysie couldn't wait to get back on her horse and just enjoy the sun. Quynn was still ready for a nap and claimed she didn't care if her horse decided to go off and eat grass. They said goodbye to Mrs. Dornoch and promised to be back at three that afternoon. Kaysie cheerfully saddled and bridled her black quarter horse gelding and practically flew onto his back once outside. Quynn plodded out a few minutes later on her dapple-gray Clydesdale. When they were out of sight of the stables, Kaysie said in a voice just above a whisper, "I brought the scroll."

Quynn nodded, strangely worried and excited at the prospect of the scroll. "The leaves aren't bugged," she said, then added as she flattened a horse fly the size of a half dollar, "Never mind."

Kaysie chuckled. "Why don't we take another look at it in the next clearing?"

The two 15-year-olds knew these trails like they were their own. Both knew that there were thick long-branched pines covering the next clearing that the two could hide underneath and still have a place to sit under the needles and examine the scroll. The horses could be allowed to eat the long grass on the other side of the trail. They were still wary of Carry's presence. They had not noticed her at the stables while they were getting their horses ready for the long ride.

The girls unrolled the parchment from its leather binding and looked over the letters once again. As they silently poured over the intricate drawings on the scroll, the two heard hoofbeats gradually coming closer and froze. Carry astride a palomino horse came into view from behind the curve in the trail behind them. The horse was going at a nice canter, catching up to the girls in their hiding place in quite a hurry. With a brief thought to the Medieval fantasy books that she loved and wondering if the strange words truly were a spell of some sort, Quynn exclaimed in a sure, strong voice, "Shirak tenkets drades kelmund sh'kanu jeeras LEVAX!"

Carry stopped her horse near the grove of trees, flew off the left side, and ran towards the girls. "NO! You don't understand the powers—!"

They heard no more of Carry's warning. The girls disappeared.

just the beginning

There was a feeling of nothingness. Neither girl could feel their bodies. The darkness surrounded them like a security blanket. The two girls had involuntarily closed their eyes and drifted on the nothingness, content to float off into the void.

The girls re-emerged an indecipherable time later, still surrounded by trees. Rubbing her eyes, Kaysie mumbled sleepily, "I had the strangest dream... We dozed off while we were taking a trail ride through the forest..."

Her words trailed off when her eyes took in the woods that had appeared before them. The forest was full of tall ancient oaks sitting close by thick cedar trees that seemed to reach for the clear sky overhead. Rich green leaves graced branches that were gently swaying in the warm breeze. Leaves mixed with the dry dirt and the occasional insect searching for its next meal on the forest floor in a motley coloration of warm and cool earth tones. But, Kaysie didn't notice the beauty of the forest. She didn't notice the perfect blue sky laced by the overhanging branches of the oak tree beside her. Her heart seemed trapped, trapped in this strange place with the world closing in around her. Kaysie had never been lost before, and chaos ruled her thoughts. Kaysie's eyes were just beginning to fill with tears. She had never felt so helpless before. There had always been ways out of situations. This was nothing like anything she had ever encountered. This wasn't the forest behind Moonstone Stables. This wasn't any place she had ever seen. Kaysie's heart began to pound in her chest as fear rose in her throat. She didn't see her best friend right away. "Quynn?"

Quynn was still snoozing on a bed of warm leaves nearby. Kaysie's voice rose as she discovered the body beside her. "Quynn!"

"Go back to bed," she mumbled.

"Um, we're not at Moonstone anymore." Kaysie's voice cracked, fear overtaking her.

"Wha- huh? What are you talking abou—" Quynn sat up slowly, and her eyes grew wide. "Um, where are we?"

"I don't know."

Instinctively, Quynn checked what they had with them: old leather backpack, the snacks, earrings, rings, a pocket watch, beaded chokers, all their clothes, a hair band each, and the parchment. Except the parchment was different. "Um, the words are gone," Kaysie said slowly, "How do we get home?"

Quynn remembered that in her books, scrolls were only usable once. She thought sarcastically at how she had always wondered what happened after the scroll was used. This wasn't exactly how Quynn had envisioned finding out the answer.

Before Quynn could come up with an answer, the two suddenly heard footsteps. Looking to the left, Quynn spied a narrow foot trail leading through the trees. The two sat perfectly still, eyes on the dirt path before them. Soon, a small man appeared walking unhurriedly down the path, his body and head just visible above the foliage. He was all in leathers, from cap to boot and had several leather pouches hanging from an ornate black leather belt. A short sword in a simple leather sheath and a long-bladed dagger hung at his waist from his belt on the opposite side. The man looked several years older then them, yet his eyes told them that they had seen more in his short lifetime than either of them could imagine.

Quynn slowly stood up, seeing Kaysie unmoving beside her. Nervously, she waved. "Um, hi, sir. We're lost, and—"

The man started and whirled around toward the direction of Quynn's voice, hand going instinctively onto the hilt of the dagger. When he noticed the girls, he clasped the hand over his heart. "By the gods, m'ladies, you'll send a man to his death. You're lost?"

He motioned for them to come over to the trail. Quynn picked up the backpack, slung it over both shoulders, and followed her best friend toward the stranger. Again, Quynn thought of her Medieval fantasy books. Leathers, lightly armored, armed with a short sword and dagger and a bow slung over a shoulder; Quynn thought quickly. A warrior of the forest from her stories. The man looked at the girls up and down, studying their clothes. He had seen women in pants before, but none like these. "Excuse me, where are my manners? I am Rilee Rayvensclaw. And you are?" he asked, bowing slightly at the waist.

"I'm Quynn Dornoch," Quynn answered, "And this is Kaysie Haggerty. We are definitely lost."

"Come with me. I'm traveling into the next town. It's not too far away."

Rilee began walking once again down the trail. The girls looked curiously at each other, shrugged, and followed.

the town of Keldon's Hill, pop. 1500

Once out of the forest, a town became visible, built in the valley of two tall, grassy hills. A high stone wall surrounded the town with four small round towers on each corner. "This is Keldon's Hill," Rilee said proudly, "I've lived here all my life."

Quynn and Kaysie exchanged quick glances. He spoke like he had been around for decades. The gate to the town was crafted of thick iron bars that reminded Kaysie of an expensive gated neighborhood. The two guards at the gate waved to Rilee as he passed through the open gate and looked curiously at the girls. Quynn and Kaysie quickly followed behind him into the town. It was just like one of Quynn's fantasy books: stone and wooden buildings intermixed with greenery and people going about their day's work. Cobblestones marked the main streets, and dirt and pebbles showed the way to less used trails and alleyways. Everyone was dressed in leathers or in thin cloth in browns and grays. Very few wore colored garments, Quynn noticed, and even then, they were in rich earthen tones.

The colors were in the shops' signs. If it weren't for them, the town would look like an old sepia-toned photograph. Bright colors showed shoes, thread spools, fish, and vegetables carved with varying skill from a hard wood. These signs were everywhere the storekeepers could place them- in windows, nailed to doors, and hanging from the rafters over the cobblestones below. Rilee led Quynn and Kaysie to a building apart from the others. Most of the buildings that they had seen were built together, like an old western gold diggers' town. This was built in the middle, around a giant round grassy space with a well in the center. The sign over this building showed a fluffy bed, or as fluffy as wood can depict, over a mug of ale, a white froth spilling over its wooden borders. Over another door nearby was a warrior clad in armor with red scales, carved like a lizard's back. Quynn recognized it as dragon scale armor, armor made from a dragon's hide, from her books and role-playing games. Rilee opened the door and made a wide sweeping motion with his arm and pointed inward. "Welcome to The Dragon Warrior. After you, m'ladies."

Wall sconces with torches firmly stuck into them dimly lit the long rectangular room. Old hammered iron chandeliers hung in a straight line from the door to the bar, like a guide, giving the room a yellow flickering glow. Thick wooden tables were placed at odd intervals. Men in armors made from leather and small linked steel slumped over the tables, drinking large mugs of ale and eating something gray and unidentifiable out of bowls. A few had actual food, looking to be some kind of cut meat and spiced potatoes. Rilee looked like a small child with a toy sword next to most of these thick men with large battle axes and broad bladed swords leaning against tables and on unused chairs. Some of the men turned to look at the two girls and grinned, showing few teeth and browned gums. Kaysie and Quynn involuntarily shuddered and walked closer to Rilee. He confidently went up to a square-shaped man at a brown-stained wooden counter surrounded by opaque glass bottles and chest-high keg barrels. Quynn thought that his man looked to be part keg himself. "These two ladies need a meal and a room for the night," Rilee said gallantly.

The large man grinned, showing that he, too, was missing several teeth, a few white spots showing through the long thick black beard. "No problem, Rilee," he said, "I'll keep an eye on 'em." The large man turned to the girls. "What's yer pleasure?"

"Um, we don't have any money," Quynn said to the man, louder than she had anticipated.

The older man laughed. "Don't ye worry. Ole Dalgrim

Silverbeard'll take care a ya, m'ladies."

With that, he called out to his right through a side door that was propped open. "Two plates uh the special! That'll be right out, m'ladies."

Rilee ushered the stunned girls to an empty table against the wall and offered them a seat on the hard wooden benches that surrounded it. Quynn and Kaysie leaned against the wood paneled wall for support. They needed to take this all in. Everything was happening so quickly. "I'll need to get you some clothes, too," they heard Rilee saying, "Then everyone won't stare as much. Where did you say you were from again? I'd really like to help you."

Quynn paused. Kaysie looked at her friend. After a pause, Quynn said, "Really far away."

"I don't understand. Beyond the Great Oceans? Over the Barkante Mountains?"

"You wouldn't believe us if we told you," Kaysie interjected.

Rilee became very serious. He leaned in over the table, loser to the two lost girls. "Try me."

Quynn sighed and looked Rilee straight in the eyes. "Magic."

"Magic."

Rilee repeated it like they had said that they had come in on the last wagon. "So, did you lose all your powers, coming here?"

He could have said, "How was the weather? I heard it rained last night."

Quynn decided to explain about the scroll, and for the first time, explained aloud the feelings that seemed connected with it. Kaysie interjected where they found it. They both retold the story of the trail ride, and of Carry coming after them. Neither mentioned anything about the time period that they were truly from, preferring instead, to pretend they were just from another area of the countryside. "And no, we never had any powers to lose. It was just this scroll," finished Quynn.

Rilee went silent, seeming to be lost in thought. Fortunately, this was the moment that the bartender decided to come over with the plates of hot, steaming food balanced on his tree-trunk arms. Quynn noticed that the big man, well, wasn't all that big. He stood a few inches under five feet, yet was built like one of the kegs behind the counter. The long black beard that hung to his waist sported a thick leather thong tied near the end of the thick mass. On the thong hung several tiny silver weapons and a single black feather that ended at his knees. Large tan boots that were worn with use and age carried the man to the table as he put the plates in front of the patrons. It was all Quynn could do from offering thanks to Thorgun, the Dwarven god in her books, but she held her tongue, for fear of looking foolish.

"By Thorgun's beard, this'll be the best meal you've had!" The dwarf shook a knotted meaty forefinger at the table, yet continued to smile at his guests.

Rilee shook his head. "Those dwarves," Rilee muttered, smiling to himself, just loud enough for the girls to hear, "You'd think that Thorgun was the only god out there."

Quynn wanted to laugh or cry, she wasn't sure which, but forced herself to look at what was set before her. It was a gray slab of meat wrapped around a large bone with the knobby ends of the bone sticking out on either end like a handle. A pile of sliced potatoes lay beside the meat. Liquid butter mixed with little black specks that she could not identify spread over the meal in a yellow blanket. A large mug of milk, or at least it looked like milk, was placed beside her plate. It smelled wonderful. When Quynn closed her eyes, she could almost see home.

The two picked up the meat like corn on the cob and took a tentative bite. It was soft and tender and delicious! Butter started to dribble down Kaysie's chin, but she quickly licked it up. The meat melted in their mouths. Neither wanted to know what the meat really was. They had never tasted anything like it, even chicken. "How's the goat?" Rilee inquired politely, stabbing a few potatoes and shoving them into his mouth.

Inwardly, the girls cringed. Each could see it on the other's face. "Very good," they chorused, trying not to choke.

"Spiced potatoes and goat leg smothered with fresh butter and spices are Dalgrim's specialty." Rilee beamed, as if he specially prepared the meal for the girls, "After this, we need to go clothes shopping. The fewer stares you ladies get, the better."

medieval fantasy

After their meal, Rilee ushered the girls back outside and into the town square. Quynn hadn't noticed how thick the darkness was in the tavern until she came through the door and into the daylight. The light of the sun seemed stark as she blinked a few times to readjust her eyes. Rilee's blur moved to the left, so she followed the shadow's movements. "I don't have any women in my life, so you will have to pick out something by yourselves. I won't be of much help," Rilee said matter-of-factly, heading towards a shop with dresses hanging in the windows.

Rilee lead them under a long awning, sheltered from the brightness of the sun with a large exaggerated triangle shaped princess' hat with flowing carved ribbons flowing down from the top. "Right this way, m'ladies," he said, again ushering them forward with a wide sweep of his arms.

Inside wasn't nearly as dark as the tavern. Large clear glass windows were set in the front of the large room, letting in the sunlight. Large chandeliers hung from the ceiling with oversized candles shoved inside small holders that shone their warm light on the patrons below. Dresses, shirts, pants, and as many accessories as the girls could think of lay neatly on tables and chairs and shelves. The flames illuminated the rich colors and sparkled off of silver accessories. Quynn didn't want to pry, but she asked, "Do you have the money for all of this?"

Rilee laughed. "Pick out what you want, Quynn. Do not worry about such things."

Kaysie and Quynn decided to start out by looking at what they liked the most - leather. Kaysie fell in love with a thick black leather belt with a beaten steel buckle. The oval buckle displayed a large pegasus, looking to be more of a draft horse than the thin, graceful Arabian that she was used to seeing, flowing around the edges with its two wings spilling into the center. Quynn discovered a similar style belt, but the image was of a silver fairy dancing through a sea of stars. Next, the two friends looked at boots. Rilee had said boots were more durable than shoes or sandals and led them to a tall dark wood shelf. On it were pair after pair of leather boots like nothing the girls had ever seen. They had been to plenty of horse shows and leather shops and flea markets to have seen handmade boots, but these took their breath away. Kaysie breathed in the soft smells of the leather. Her eyes began to tear. Quickly, she banished all thoughts of home and concentrated on finding a pair of boots she liked. "May I help you, m'ladies?"

Kaysie's heart almost stopped as she was startled out of her reverie. Quynn seemed not to have noticed. "These boots," Quynn said nonchalantly, pointing.

Quynn took down a pair of boots that looked to have been made from scraps of different brown-hued leather and handed them to the large woman behind them. She was dressed in a sand-colored cloth dress under a tight bodice that was squeezing out more than just cleavage. A large oatmeal-colored knitted kerchief was tied over her head, and the ends hung past her neck. Leather tools peeked over the edges of pockets sewn into an old beige apron that at one point in its existence, may have been white. She looked at the boots, then at Quynn's feet. She put the pair back, and as Quynn was about to protest, she took down a pair similar to the original, and said, "Here. These will fit better."

Quynn sat on a nearby chair and tried them on. They were the most comfortable things she had ever put on her feet. Kaysie was looking at her expectantly, holding another pair of boots. These were black with faint black designs stitched into them. Rilee was busy looking at other styles of boot. "These are really comfortable," Quynn whispered, "Try yours."

Kaysie couldn't believe it. She had spent a good deal of money on her riding boots, and these felt like slippers. She did not want to know how much these would cost, but she kept her mouth shut.

The two walked around the store with the boots still on for awhile longer. Soon, they had two oatmeal-brown dresses and two bodices, one a deep brown, the other a deep red. They also managed to talk Rilee into letting them pick out a pair of brown leather pants, as neither could imagine wearing a dress for long periods of time. It took a lot of talking and a lot of looking, but they both found what the pants that they wanted. It laced up the front where a zipper would go on jeans and had a similar lacing on the sides so boots could fit underneath. The two whispered that they felt as though they had stepped into a Renaissance Festival, but this was real. Rilee only handed the woman two silver-colored coins for everything, something the girls couldn't fathom. Then, their new friend showed the girls a place to change. "When you need help with the bodices, let Seryna know!"

Lovely, Quynn thought, *I'm gonna get squeezed like her…*

And squeezed she was. Right before she thought she would pass out from lack of air, Seryna tied the bow on top of the bodice. Quynn could definitely not slouch now! Kaysie laughed at her friend until Seryna cut her short. "Your turn, m'lady." The two walked out of the store, backpack filled with their old clothes, standing ramrod straight, Quynn silently snickering at her best friend, while Kaysie pretended to glower.

Rilee handed the girls three empty brown leather pouches and told them to put them on their belt through the strings. "These are for you," he said smiling, "To hold all your valuables."

"We don't have any valuables here," Kaysie said, confused.

"Oh, yes, you do," Rilee said, "Are those amethyst earrings and necklaces you are wearing?"

Quynn nodded, looking at Kaysie for help. She shrugged at her confused friend. "Those are worth more than gold here," Rilee said, making sure no one was near, and leading the girls to a long bench near the well, "You girls are as rich as the king."

Certainly, Kaysie thought with a bit of sarcasm and a big smile. *Why not?*

It was getting late, but Quynn begged to look around some more, curious about exploring this medieval-fantasy-like town straight form her stories. Rilee agreed, but made sure she remembered where the room was. He took Kaysie back to The Dragon Warrior, while Quynn began to explore her new surroundings.

She remembered her books back home as she wandered the cobblestone streets. Everything fit, from the well in the middle of town to the guard towers posted at each corner. She half expected a goblin at the next intersection. Quynn wondered that since she had met a dwarf, if halflings and elves and gnomes also existed. The thought excited her, as she thought of all the questions that she longed to ask.

The sky was turning a dark blue, with faint oranges and pinks dotting the edges. Quynn knew she needed to return to The Dragon Warrior soon. As Quynn walked down the cobblestone streets back to the inn, she realized that it was practically deserted. And it was the "practically" that scared her. All those thoughts of her stories and what may be out there were beginning to make her shiver. The street was dimly lit with candles on high posts, barely illuminating a small yellow circle below. Alleyways were dark portals to Hell. Dark doorways led to worlds beyond this one. Shadows were the ogres of legend. A chill went up Quynn's spine. She had that sinking feeling that someone was following her, watching her every move. Thoughts swam in her mind: *Run!* said one, *Run as fast as you can!* Just as another contradicted it: *Whatever it is can catch you; don't be silly— you can't hurt whatever it is. You're unarmed. I wish Kaysie were here,* piped up another thought.

Quynn tried to calm herself, though her legs felt less confident about walking. Quynn heard a footstep. Just one, like soft leather on stone. So, my murderer is wearing sole-less shoes, Quynn thought, then, so what? Like I'll be able to tell the police after I've been stabbed? There was another footstep. And another, like the person decided that moving quietly was too much trouble in a deserted street. Quynn could see the warrior clad in red dragonscale armor that denoted where The Dragon Warrior Inn stood silent under the slowly setting sun. Instinctually, she began to try and find a place to hide. An alley was a few feet ahead. She ducked into the darkness and behind a large crate. Quynn closed her eyes and tried to breathe. Then, a warm hand appeared on her shoulder. Quynn's breath stuck in her throat, unable to scream, while her heart savored its final beats. For what seemed like long enough for the sun to start peaking out from over the tops of the trees, nothing happened. "Please don't scream, m'lady," a soft male voice pleaded, "I won't hurt you. Really."

Quynn recognized the accent as something she had heard before, but could not place it. She opened her eyes. There was a man, about her age and about six inches taller, standing in a loose black cloth shirt, black leather pants, and black boots with a small dagger in a leather sheath hanging at his waist, barely visible behind a large plain black belt pouch. Dark brown hair lay in chaos around his ears and chiseled face. His green eyes looked pleadingly at Quynn, like a puppy that is certain it will be scolded. The man spoke again. "I am Terryn Moonshade," and he bowed low.

"Quynn Dornoch," she said, just above a whisper.

Terryn nodded. "I know. Someone is looking for you and your friends. I cannot tell you too much here. These old stones have ears."

He looked disgustedly at the building as if it had just offended his heritage. "Meet me at the edge of the forest next sun when the sun is at its peak. I will see you long before you see me," he added mysteriously.

With that, the dark-clothed figure disappeared into the night.

pieces of enlightenment

Quynn was visibly shaken. How could anyone know her and Kaysie were there, wherever they were? He seemed nice enough, but people could be deceiving. And his disappearing act scared her. How did he do that? With all her knowledge of fantasy and Medieval life, it didn't make a whole lot of sense- unless... She sighed, remembering her role-playing games- thief. Quynn wasn't quite sure if that piece of information made her any happier, though she knew from her books that not all thieves were bad news.

When Quynn had collected her thoughts, she jogged back to the inn. She waved to the barkeep and threw him a wish of well being, including his beard and Thorgun. She got the desired effect. The dwarf's eyes grew large, in part with surprise and in part with admiration, pleased that this human girl knew of his people's customs. Quynn smiled and continued up the stairs to the rooms. She found their room easily and knocked three times. After a moment, Kaysie opened the door. "Aren't you a bit late?" She looked worried.

"I need to talk to you," Quynn whispered between her teeth.

Then louder, she added, "I'm fine. I just got caught up in the leather store and lost track of time."

Rilee barely nodded. He was pouring over the scroll, sans the writing and symbols that brought them there, like he had waited until the last moment to study for a physics test. He sat at a low, wide dresser as if it were a desk, seated in a high-backed wooden chair, his hair barely visible above his dark brown cloak.

Quynn took her best friend over to a corner of the room by the window and whispered her adventures. Rilee shifted only once, entranced by the paper in front of him. Then, Quynn announced her theory. "My books. Everything sounds like the stories in my books. Not necessarily the people, but the situations; the background." Quynn struggled with the right words to show her best friend what she was thinking. "Not that it answers any questions—it seems to bring up more."

Kaysie shrugged. She knew little of medieval fantasy or history. The closest she had ever gotten was looking at the pictures in her friend's role-playing game books. Kaysie voiced her fears to Quynn. "So, those weren't fiction stories you were always reading, were they? Someone didn't make it all up. Those were real."

Quynn slowly nodded, looking out of the corner of her eye at Rilee. Still studying for that physics test, she thought. She sighed. "Found anything in there?"

Rilee looked up, obviously startled. "I need some more time. Uh, I'm trying to recall this tower. I think I may have heard tales from some of my adventures."

He went back to studying the paper. When Rilee had lifted himself up, Quynn noticed that several thick books were open underneath him. They were open to detailed ink drawings of people and towers. One looked to be a wizard. Then, suddenly, they were covered again, as if Rilee didn't want the girls to cheat off of his physics test.

Quynn and Kaysie let their new friend pour over the parchment awhile longer. Soon, they were restless. They wanted answers. Quynn thought she knew a few of them, but it still sounded foolish that her books weren't just fantasy stories after all.

Quietly, Quynn walked over to Rilee and stood behind him. Carefully, she stood on her toes, craning to see over his shoulders and around his head. If Rilee noticed, he didn't say or do anything. Quynn caught glimpses of what looked like the tower in the drawing on the parchment. The view was different, but she recognized the balcony that seemed to be the center of the scroll's picture. Next to the ink drawing in one of the books that Rilee was immersed in was a drawing of what looked to be a mage. "Roustin Blackfyre" was written in perfect calligraphy below the image of the wizard that was carefully detailed and almost looked real.

Then, a strange feeling came over the young girl. Someone was behind her. She almost screamed. The warmth from whoever was behind her moved slightly, causing a board to squeak. Quynn jumped out of the way, fearing a long-bladed knife going for her back once again. Rilee absent-mindedly turned around to see what the commotion was. He raised an eyebrow at the girls. Kaysie tried to move out of the way, but almost ran into Quynn. Before Rilee could form a question, Quynn blurted, "Kaysie! What are you doing?!"

Her heart was pounding against her chest. Kaysie looked sheepish. "I wanted to see what was going on. I don't know what, um, you know. I believe you, but…"

Rilee spit it out. "What are you talking about? Do you know something, Quynn?"

Silence. She still felt foolish for thinking the fantasy books were real, despite the circumstances pointing out otherwise. They were both staring at her. "Um, this may sound crazy, but, um, I used to read these stories, um, before I came here, and um," Quynn paused, gaining the courage to say what was on her mind, then continued quickly, "I think they are true."

Quynn braced herself for the laughter she was sure would follow. Silence again. Rilee was looking at her more intently now. She felt like she was about to be interrogated. "What do you know?"

It was a harsh command, not really a question, but Quynn forgave him. "I don't know this Roustin, but I understand the land, the customs, the religion. You see, uh, we have these books, back where I came from, and I thought they were just stories."

Quynn continued to tell the man what she knew of the dwarves, elves, halflings, and humans, and the gods that were worshiped. It was everything she had read and enjoyed. She couldn't believe it was real. Half way through the explanation, she sat on the straw mattress and spoke to the wall. Her mind was still spinning, and she needed a solid familiar object to talk to.

Kaysie started to feel again like a third wheel. She had never read these books, had never lived in this land... How could she possibly be useful? Yeah, she thought, I've won the Tri-County Horse Show Best of Show for three years running, topped the western riding classes, and gone to the State Fair through 4-H for six years. She had stopped listening to her best friend. Kaysie had one talent: horseback riding. How did these people get around? On horseback! Suddenly, she smiled to herself and continued to listen to the history of this strange land, intent on learning more.

Rilee looked at Quynn intently the whole time she was speaking, even when she directed her speech at the wall. "I don't know how you know so much, if you are not from here. Some of the things you have mentioned have not been spoken of. But, I still think more research is needed on this tower," he added and sighed, like he knew he really needed to study for that physics test.

Quynn paused. She contemplated on telling Rilee about Terryn. No, she decided, she would be better off seeing this man alone. When you are fifteen, Quynn decided, you don't need a baby-sitter.

sketches

Quynn had taken some parchment from Rilee's stash and a few pieces of charcoal that he wasn't using with her on the premise of drawing in the woods. Quynn claimed she needed to be alone. The rolled parchment was tucked in her belt and the few pieces of charcoal lay at the bottom of a thin leather pouch, tied at her hip. Quynn glanced around nervously for the young man she had seen. She was more scared that he really would see her first and scare her intentionally. Quynn was beginning to be rather wary of being startled senseless. She paused for a moment on the edge of the forest. She heard nothing, but the soft birdsong and a light breeze rustling the leaves. Quynn wandered through the outskirts of the wood, noticing the textures on the trees and how the sunlight reflected off of the dark green leaves, dangling from thick branches. Quynn found a particularly interesting oak tree with a triangular crack starting halfway up the tree and spreading to the base. It was leaning to the left, as if trying to support the weight of the hole. She sat against a large cedar and began to sketch the interesting scene.

Quynn was really getting into the soft details of the leaves when she heard a noise, and she froze. There was suddenly a man-shaped shadow over her drawing. Her left hand immediately clutched the handle of the long-bladed dagger that Rilee had insisted upon giving her. "I told you I would see you first, m'lady. I didn't know you could draw so well."

Quynn eyed the figure standing above her. It was Terryn. She let out a breath she didn't know she was holding. "Thank you," she said, calming down, "Could you not scare me like that?" Quynn added in a mildly annoyed tone.

"Sorry. I didn't realize you would be armed, m'lady," Terryn said apologetically.

Quynn sighed, put away her charcoal, and relaxed her grip on the blade. "So, what exactly is going on?"

"Roustin Blackfyre knows you are here. He's learning the powers you possess," Terryn whispered, after glancing around at the trees, "I cannot say too much. Even the birds may be spies for him. Be careful what you say and to whom. I am slowly learning the secrets he is withholding. I am close to him, you might say."

"How? How are you close to him? What do you do, when you're not sneaking around?"

Quynn spoke softly, and he back to her. They paused in their conversation, when a crow landed on a branch above them and stared with coal-black eyes. After what seemed like an hour, the crow spread its black wings and flew away. The two continued to talk in hushed tones, until Terryn said that he could tell her no more at this time. "Meet me here again as the sun sets for the seventh time, as the seventh moon rises above the treetops. I shall be able to tell you more at that time. Good day, m'lady."

She watched as he disappeared in to the woods before sketching a bit more to set up the intent of drawing something out here, though her mind swam at her newfound knowledge. Then, she packed her tools and headed again for town.

When Quynn got back to the tavern, the first thing she did was eat. It was the best gray mush she'd ever eaten. Quynn figured it was leftovers from the day before, as the taste of the melted butter came through on the tougher of the gray lumps. Quynn was dying for a cheeseburger. She tried not to think about it as she wolfed down the Mystery Lunch. Inside, she was bursting to tell Rilee and Kaysie about Terryn. Things were slowly piecing together, even though this new information seemed to be a door leading to an even bigger room of mystery.

Soon enough, Quynn was upstairs and inside the room they were all sharing. Rilee had gone for more books. Kaysie had no idea where he was getting all of these tomes. She had remained behind, though, hoping her best friend would show up soon. She felt uncomfortable in this setting. Kaysie missed her home more than she would admit. Kaysie wanted the funniest things at times. She wanted a picture of her mother. She wanted an old teddy bear. She even missed her little brother. Kaysie was sitting on the bed, staring out onto the unfamiliar landscape. Tears were just thinking about starting when Quynn came through the door. She jumped a little at the noise, then settled back against the pillows. "Girl, have I got a story for you," Quynn announced.

"You saw your boyfriend again?" Kaysie managed a mischievous grin, thinking of when her friend first met Terryn on the street.

Quynn gave her a look. "I did see Terryn again. And he's not my boyfriend! He's the fourth of seven children. All of them work for this Roustin that Rilee was looking at in the books. The mom almost died after the second child, and Roustin saved her. The dad was very grateful. He also wanted to have his wife possess an elf's long lifespan, like his. Well, the family got enslaved, kind of. Roustin took the parents soon after the last child was born, saying that he was going to help. No one knows where they are. The children are servants of this wizard in his tower. It's the youngest child, Sevyn, who is slowly learning Roustin's ways. She had started to pretend to be obsessed with learning to be a wizard herself when she was very young. Except now, Sevyn's really showing talent in the ancient arts. It's Sevyn who's telling her older brother all she learns about Roustin and could find us a way home."

By the time Quynn had finished her story, her voice had risen in volume, like an exuberant child relaying something exciting that happened at school. Kaysie's jaw hung wide open while her friend spoke. It had seemed so impossible before. Maybe this new life wasn't permanent. Hope crept up on Kaysie, but she fought it. *I shouldn't have too much faith*, she thought, *I'll get hurt in the end.* "You should tell Rilee before he checks out every book in the library," she finally said and smiled, glancing at the small piles of books on the desk.

Quynn stifled a laugh. "Yes, Kaysie." She sighed, thinking of how she'd have to repeat the story again.

Rilee came in not too long after their conversation, or rather a pile of books with legs came in, several minutes after Quynn completed telling her story to her best friend. The pile leaned backwards, then lurched forwards as the books landed with a resounding thud on the desk. A few on top kept sliding, but were stopped short of falling off completely by Kaysie's outstretched hand. Rilee seemed out of breath. "Thank you," he said, sighing.

Before he could do anything else, Quynn spoke up. "There's something important I need to talk to you about."

"Hmm?" Rilee said, beginning to sit down onto the cushioned chair that now had his permanent imprint.

"About Roustin Blackfyre."

That got his attention. Rilee sat down with his left arm draped over the back of the chair, staring at Quynn, questions written all over his face. "I know how to find him and get information about him without you emptying the library of its contents," she clarified, "I spoke with Terryn Moonshade."

Quynn proceeded to tell him everything, except she left out the parts about Terryn scaring her twice. Rilee never said a word, only nodded a few times in wonderment. When she was finished, Rilee added, "I can tell you more about the tower. Well, it's not really just a tower. It's more of a small castle, but the west tower is so big, that it's always been called that, it seems. That balcony that is on the scroll is halfway up this tower and leads into the main chamber- the study, if you will, where the experimentation lab is. Roustin is a necromancer—" at the funny look from Kaysie, not at the astonished and slowly paling face of Quynn, he explained, "A wizard who specializes in the living and dead, but mostly undead. It could be how he brought Hailea Moonshade—the mother—back."

Kaysie paled at the thought of those old slow moving mummies from bad b-movies plodding after her relentlessly. Quynn slowly sat down on the straw mattress, shaking. After all her books, she did not want to be a zombie; or a skeleton; or a wraith; or caught in a grisly spell. Quynn knew that she knew better than her best friend what they night face. "So," he continued, "The tower is east of here, a few days' travel. It's tucked away in the forest off of an animal trail off of the main road. I have read that it's hard to spot amongst the dozens of other animal trails. But it seems we will have a guide soon."

Kaysie's stomach twisted and churned, and she didn't think it was the Mystery Lunch that Dalgrim had served her.

the cooking lesson

Kaysie decided that it was time to learn how to live in this area. She had it in her mind that she was never leaving this place, and food would be a great place to start. First thing in the morning, Kaysie decided to show Dalgrim how to make a one of her favorite foods. Quynn wasn't the only one dying for a cheeseburger.

The fifteen-year-old marched up to the dwarf right after breakfast. Dalgrim was startled, understandably, as the young girl had barely said a word to anyone, let alone him. "I would like to teach you how to make something," she said, meeker than she intended.

It didn't seem to matter that she was six inches taller than the dwarf—he was still intimidating. Dalgrim was in brown leather pants covered with a wide oatmeal-colored apron and a dark red cloth shirt. Wooden cooking utensils and at least a half dozen pouches of varying sizes hung from thick leather cords on an old cracked black leather belt that fit snuggly around the old dwarf's waist. Dalgrim's long black hair was pulled back with a thick black leather strip, and the silver trinkets were still tied tightly to the obsidian colored beard. It was the only part of him that seemed well kept, though. The rest was covered in sweat, grease, and age. Dalgrim smiled. Kaysie shuddered.

She cleared her throat. "I need ground beef and a few spices," Kaysie said, trying to sound like she wasn't nervous and knew exactly what she was doing.

"Beef?" The old dwarf looked confused.

"Cow meat." Kaysie clarified.

"Got goat," Dalgrim said gruffly, though trying to be helpful. Another inward shudder. "Ok."

They walked back to the kitchen, and Dalgrim lead her into the cellar. He came back with a handful of ground meat wrapped in thin paper. Kaysie took the contents and made six patties out of them and mixed in some salt, pepper, and garlic. "Cheese?" she asked timidly, worried he'd come back with something inedible.

Sighing, the dwarf went back to the cellar and came back with a small wheel of yellow cheese wrapped in a thick opaque paper. Kaysie took a knife and made several uneven slices. She put these slices on top of the meat. She thought quickly about what else she needed. "A tray of some sort. A rectangle, preferably."

Dalgrim bent down, which seemed to take some effort, grabbed a tray off of a lower shelf, and handed it to the human girl. Kaysie arraigned the patties on the tray and put the whole thing in the oven. Then, she thought of something important. She had no idea how long to keep them there. She showed no fear. "When it's done, you have a cheeseburger. Do you have any round rolls?"

The old dwarf looked rather confused, but did as he was asked. He produced a bag of thick round rolls for Kaysie from the cellar. She cut them in half with a serrated knife and waited. She made sure to check on her concoction every five minutes. Soon, they looked to be done. It smelled wonderful. Kaysie almost cried as the homesickness poured over her. She swallowed a few times before putting the burger on the roll. Ketchup. Pickles. Did he even know what ketchup was? Kaysie dared try. "Ketchup," she said.

Dalgrim looked at the girl like she had just sprouted wings and pronounced herself a pixie. "Um, tomato sauce and spices," she fumbled.

Dalgrim smiled and handed her a long cylindrical tin can covered like a beer stein. She inhaled the contents. Perfect.

Quynn couldn't believe it. Neither could a few of the patrons. The cheeseburgers were a hit, but they had to be made smaller if the meat was going to last. Kaysie was going to be occupied for awhile, and Dalgrim was going to be very happy with the week's profits.

Moonshade

Now that Quynn knew that she would be well fed, she took the opportunity to explore the town. Market Day was being held along the main roads in the town, and it spread to encompass the town's square. She wanted to check it out. Since her amethyst was so expensive here, Quynn decided to first go to the jewelers.

She wandered into a building tucked away behind the moneychanger's, trying to look nonchalant. Quynn glanced around at the cases, astounded at the quality of the jewelry and the creativity of the craftsman. While she was staring intently at a silver bracelet that had intricate, almost Celtic knot-like, webbing between two thin silver bands, a melodious voice interrupted her thoughts. "Would you like to see something, m'lady?"

She glanced up, startled, to see a young woman, probably her age, standing directly in front of her on the other side of the counter. "Oh, um, I ah, wanted to see what this was worth."

Quynn removed an amethyst-beaded bracelet that had cost her five dollars back home. There were fifteen beads the size of her pinky nail. The woman's eyes grew to the size of the bracelet. She said slowly, "M'lady, would you like that in jewelry or coin?"

Quynn thought for a moment. In her books, gems were easier to carry, depending on the worth. Though, coin made one look less conspicuous. "Can I have both?" she asked.

"Yes, m'lady. That'll be 1500 gold pieces, by my reasoning. Is there anything you were looking at?"

Quynn pointed to the bracelet. The woman took it out of the case and let Quynn try it on. The thick bands fit around her wrist perfectly. The woman beamed. "That's my finest piece."

"You did this?" Quynn was astounded, "How much?"

"Two-hundred gold. It's silver," she said modestly.

Quynn gave the woman two of the beads off of the elastic band. Sounds of the market began to float in. She had to get moving soon. "Can I just have coin and some smaller gems for one of these?"

"Yes, m'lady," and gave Quynn several small gems, 100 gold pieces, and a small pouch of silver coins.

Quynn put the money in a fur-lined pouch hanging in front of her like a Scottish sporran. She put the rest of the beads in the pouch, too. "Thank you," Quynn said, excusing herself from the woman.

Quynn readjusted her eyes to the summer sun quicker than she had before. The colors of the market contrasted with the dullness of the rest of the town caught her eyes through a narrow alleyway as she made her way toward the throngs of people. Quynn kept an arm and an eye on her pouch. I have read too many books, she thought, but that didn't keep her eye and arm from protecting her money. Booths were set up on both sides of the cobblestone main street, keeping the normal horse and cart traffic away from the wares. It reminded Quynn of the last Renaissance Festival she had attended, except no one was acting, and there was no one wandering about in jeans and t-shirts. She watched several performers, including a juggler and a storyteller. Stories of knights in shining armor and the elves of the deepest caves swam in her head, as she tried to remember every detail. She knew that she had heard some of these tales before, as Quynn remembered a few of the tales from her fantasy books. Too bad Kaysie was missing this.

Everyone ignored her, even people she has seen before. She was beginning to feel lonely, despite the large crowd. Quynn realized she had pretty much seen everything, when she noticed one more person, standing on the fringes of the town near a small side gate. The girl looked to be Quynn's age, but she was dressed in a way that she hadn't seen here before. A leather triangle-shaped cloth hung over her front, and brown leather pants clung to her legs. Quynn was momentarily jealous, as she had not had a chance to wear her pants, and it had not taken her long to become sick of dresses. Feathers poked out of her hair, seemingly at random, yet making a beautiful pattern of color. But what really caught Quynn's eye was the animal at her feet. It was a medium-sized silver wolf. The creature was staring at Quynn with intense blue eyes, but was not growling or showing any aggression. The girl waved slightly at Quynn. Quynn felt a little embarrassed, thinking she was staring a little too long. "I'm sorry," Quynn said, coming a little closer, "I didn't mean to stare."

The girl nodded, as dark auburn hair shifted in the breeze. Quynn saw something then that almost made her hug the figure in front of her. It was an elf. Or maybe a half-elf. Her features weren't as pointed as the elves she had read about and loved to play in her games, yet the pointed ears seemed to flow up her head like water around rocks in a stream. Quynn knew in an instant that she was older than she looked. And she had a strange resemblance to Terryn. She decided to try. "I'm Quynn," she said, "Quynn Dornoch."

"I am Breyanathesti Moonshade, but call me Breyah," she answered.

"Oh, my god," Quynn wanted to exclaim, "Oh, this is so cool. You're an elf. Or half-elf. I have so many questions I'd love to ask you right now."

Instead of looking foolish by talking, though, Quynn managed to look foolish by standing there with her mouth open. Breyah smiled, then waved half-heartedly, like when someone is staring at you, and you want them to know you're looking back. "You're Terryn's sister," Quynn managed to spit out.

"Yes," Breyah said softly. Quynn thought her voice sounded like a songbird. "A younger sister."

Quynn nodded, unable to say anymore to someone that she wished to ask thousand questions. "Terrynoust has described you well," Breyah said, smiling, then added as if thinking of an old conversation, "You *are* cute."

Quynn flushed as red as her hair. "Thank you. Uh, he said that?"

Breyah nodded, the wolf circling through her legs, seeming both uncomfortable and restless, like it wanted to be moving again, yet wouldn't leave her side. "Laeryna seems uneasy, yet I have warnings for you, young human. Be wary of Roustin. He may be an old man, yet he possesses strong magic within. My sister's magic is strong, but not nearly as strong as Roustin's. Be careful."

Breyah looked like a mother warning her child about thieves in the night, her eyes pleading with Quynn. She nodded and tried to look brave. "Yes. I will. We all will."

As Breyah turned to leave, Quynn spoke up. "Are you a druid?"

Breyanathesti looked puzzled at the question. "I am half-elven and of the forest," she said, "I do not know this 'druid.' My silver wolf and I practice the ways of the forest."

Yes, Quynn thought, in her books, this half-elf would be labeled a druid, patterned after the ancient Celts, mixed with a bit of magic and legend. That would mean that all the Moonshades were half-elven. Thoughts were rushing into Quynn's brain as Breyah waved once again and disappeared into the trees around the town.

Quynn quickly jogged back in the direction of the Dragon Warrior Inn and Tavern. Quynn briefly thought that when she got back to the inn that she would write down all the questions she ever had for elves. Maybe this Moonshade family could answer them. Her next thought was, *Wait until I tell Kaysie that we're dealing with half-elves!* Quynn smiled to herself. Would Kaysie be nearly as excited as she was? She slowed to a walk, as she came to the larger concentration of people at the market. Coming out of the congestion, Quynn practically skipped to the inn, more focused on the prospect of new races than with her current danger.

Quynn waved happily to the dwarf, who was drying a large pewter mug and nodded once at the human girl, then she ran upstairs. Well, as much as one can run in a dress. Ecstatic as she was, she didn't notice at first the serious looks on Kaysie and Rilee's faces, and that there were more than two people in the room. Quynn stopped suddenly two steps inside the room as her smile vanished from her face. "What's going on, guys?" she said, slipping into 21st century slang.

Before anyone could answer, a low growl came from under the desk. Her feet frozen to the ground, Quynn glanced to her right. Two blue eyes glowed in the shadow of the desk, then, a head peeked out. The silver wolf trotted over to Quynn and flopped on her feet. Laeryna was pretty heavy, but Quynn was too flattered at the attention to notice. She quickly regained her composure. The group managed a smile, as Quynn slowly bent her knees and stroked the wolf. "It seems my wolf likes you," Breyah said with a hint of amusement.

"We need to leave now," said a shadow that looked like it could be Terryn, "Sevyn needs us."

Rilee finally looked up. He had everything shoved into three backpacks. Kaysie could only think of how all her and Quynn's worldly belongings fit into two backpacks. She shouldered the one with her clothes and a few pouches of dried food and tried to look like she was ready for adventure.

the dark journey to Blackshroud

Kaysie was scared. A lump in her stomach turned over and over and grew larger with every passing second. She wasn't sure which she wanted more: to wake up from this dream or to inhale a bottle of Tums.

She was glad that they could go on horseback. She had a plain brown gelding with a brown mane and tail, not the exotic-looking black Arab gelding with the shiny black mane and tail she rented back home, but she didn't care. Kaysie was glad to feel the rhythmic plodding of a horse under her again. It seemed more real than this Dali-esque place.

Rilee was trying his best to teach Kaysie and Quynn how to use a short bow. Every time they stopped, they would practice shooting at a particular place on a tree along the dirt trail. Quynn had done it a few times with the plastic bows from Renaissance fairs, but had never even seen a real short bow. It felt good in her hands, one feeling the curved wood and her fingers feeling the tightening of the thin, strong string. It was Kaysie who decided that she wanted to learn while her horse was still moving. She quickly learned to hold the horse still, her training coming in handy. She silently thanked Carry for her loud instruction. The Moonshades were generally silent, unless spoken to, though Breyah smiled a lot at the girls' bow lessons.

The first early evening was filled with more short bow lessons. They were getting down the basics; now, they needed to do the aiming and firing more quickly. Breyah worked with Quynn, while Rilee helped Kaysie. Terryn said he'd keep his head down.

Turns were taken keeping a watch over the party that night. A large oak overlooked the small camp, and Breyah took first watch from up in its thick branches. She seemed to blend into the leaves. Kaysie tried to sleep, but her brain wouldn't let her. Thoughts bounded around like a runaway train through her head. *What have I gotten myself into?* was the biggest question, then, *Why couldn't we just stay where we were? Oh, we have to help these people, but why can't we help them from a distance?* Kaysie was still awake when Breyah came down from the tree, and Rilee took her place, except he decided to sit on the ground, not on a branch. Finally, Kaysie drifted off to sleep, absently swatting away flies from her head.

Morning found the coarse blanket that had been neatly placed on top of Kaysie twisted around her legs, and the smells of dried fruit drifted by her nose. Yuck, she thought, but her stomach told her she'd better eat. "Why can't we cook something?" Kaysie tried not to sound whiny as she tried to straighten her hair with a few fingers.

Terryn smiled. "You want to attract every wandering critter in the area?"

"No," she said, quietly, as she munched on the fruit flavored leather.

"Bow lessons on the other side of this tree!" Rilee called.

"Fun, fun, fun!" Quynn muttered, grinning sarcastically, trying to get her friend to stop frowning.

It worked. "Come on," Kaysie smiled, "We have to learn something useful here."

Rilee had Kaysie mount her horse with the quiver of arrows over one shoulder and the bow in her hand. Quynn stood to the side with Rilee. "Let's practice firing while the horse is moving," he said, "Aim at that pine."

Kaysie took a deep breath and nudged her horse into a walk, something she had done thousands of times. Carefully, she guided it with her legs while she aimed at the chosen target. The arrow whistled through the air following the faint sound of the string returning to its original position. The arrow lodged into the base of the tree. Again. A bit higher, this time. Kaysie turned her horse around and came at the target again. The arrow flew into the center of the trunk. She was grinning now, feeling a bit more confidant. "Do that again," Rilee said, showing her how to aim more consistently.

Kaysie shot at the tree again. "Better!" he said, smiling, then turning to his right, "Quynn?"

Quynn stood and aimed at the tree. She aimed and let the arrow go, and it flew into the trunk at an angle near the bottom. "Not bad," Rilee sounded pleased, "Now straighten out your arm, and don't pull back so hard."

Again, Quynn aimed and shot another arrow. It landed right next to Kaysie's on the tree trunk. Quynn beamed. Suddenly, a low growling behind them caught Rilee, Quynn, and Kaysie's attention. It sounded like Laeryna, but it was deeper, and there were more. Kaysie's heart rose into her throat. Wolves. Slowly, she turned around. Her horse was getting restless. She tried to control him. Terryn already had a long sword drawn and ready. Breyah had a long curved scimitar. Rilee drew back the bowstring, arrow notched and ready, and said quietly to the girls, "Target practice."

A small pack of thin wolves had cornered the rest of the group against the large oak tree and were circling, looking for a good point of attack, growling threateningly if someone moved. Rilee silently walked to the right side of the tree, bow drawn, and arrow ready. Quynn and Kaysie went left; arrows ready to be loosened. The wolves were snarling at their friends until Terryn swiped at one with the tip of his short sword, tearing a gash down its right side. The battle had begun.

The injured wolf made a lunge for Terryn's throat. Without thinking, Quynn pulled back on the bowstring and loosed an arrow in one fluid motion, and the wolf sprouted an arrow underneath its front leg as it jumped in the air. It fell with a resounding thud on the dirt. Its two companions paused for a moment too long. Breyah slashed at the wolf in front of her with her sword, wounding its shoulder, and Terryn sunk his short sword halfway into the remaining wolf. It twitched a few times, then slowly slid off the blade and into the dirt. Kaysie trotted her horse around and took aim at the wounded animal. The arrow lodged deep in the animal's side, and it tried to take Breyah's knee with it with a fierce bite, but she moved swiftly out of the way. They all breathed for a few moments, as Quynn and Kaysie looked at each other and grinned. They had done it.

Kaysie was feeling pretty confident, if a little breathless, after the short battle. Quynn was practically outshining the sun. Terryn kept shaking his head. Breyah grinned at the girls. Laeryna licked at a nonexistent wound and looked at Quynn with sorrowful eyes. "She just wants sympathy," Breyah said softly, as the wolf continued to look pleadingly at the human girl.

"It's ok. I'll pet her," she said grinning, sitting beside the oversized dog.

Laeryna flopped on her lap, underbelly in the air, paws helpfully pulled back. At that, everyone decided that it was time for a short break. They stretched their muscles and let the horses graze on the thick green grass, as Quynn rubbed the wolf's belly.

Soon, they were moving again, and the two girls were practicing controlling their horses without reins as they aimed at various targets.

Only the sounds of the hooves striking the ground and the sporadic song of birds broke the silence that surrounded the group. There were more hills now, and trees seemed to come up out of nothing as they crested grassy hills. Quynn wanted desperately to ask Breyah all her questions, but she was embarrassed. They sounded so silly when she thought about someone asking her the same questions. She took a deep breath. Breyah is in the front. I can maneuver over to her; question her without everyone hearing, she thought bravely.

Terryn thought about Quynn more and more. There were so many questions he wanted to ask her. They sounded so silly when he thought about them that he never spoke up. *Maybe I can maneuver over to her, since she's in the back, so no one else will hear me.*

Suddenly, there was a shift in the marching order. Rilee and his horse rode silently in front, confused as to where everyone disappeared. Kaysie realized that Quynn was no longer beside her and nearly panicked. She almost ran over Laeryna, when she told her horse to stop and back up. Breyah successfully backed up her horse and tried to observe what was happening from the right side of the group. Quynn lost sight of Breyah and nearly went headlong into Terryn as he approached her. It was Kaysie who stopped the confusion by laughing. Hard. So hard that tears began streaming from her eyes and her stomach began to hurt. Everyone stopped and looked at Kaysie, bewildered looks on their faces. Then, Quynn began to laugh nervously. Terryn smiled. Breyah covered her head with her left hand and began shaking. A smile was visible through the hand, though no noise emanated from her. Rilee exchanged smiles with Terryn. "You do realize that I don't know where I'm going. One of you—" he pointed at Breyah and Terryn "—is going to have to lead this expedition, not me."

Kaysie recovered, but continued to chuckle to herself out of nervousness and exhaustion. Breyah rode to the front, after exchanging a private glance with her brother. Terryn rode up beside Quynn, yet stayed silent until the party began to move again. "So, where are you from again, m'lady?"

His voice was soft, yet clear. Quynn doubted anyone else heard him. "Uh, far away," she answered.

"What did you do there? I mean…" he trailed off.

Quynn thought for a moment on how to word her answer. "I rode horses," she said slowly, "I went to school."

She regretted that last statement, but she couldn't take it back. How was she to explain that a girl went to school? "Magic?" Terryn asked casually.

Quynn sighed inwardly. "I learned history and writing and reading," she finally said, hoping that he would drop it before she let something slip about the future. She changed the subject, hoping he wouldn't question her mistake. "Kaysie and I got ribbons and awards for our horseback riding." She wanted to add "money," but didn't want to do conversions of dollars to gold. Quynn didn't know what they were anyway.

"You two are pretty good riders," Terryn said, then felt dumb for saying it.

It gave Quynn the opportunity to ask some dumb questions. They spoke of elves for most of the day, ignoring everyone else. Rilee quietly seethed that Quynn wasn't learning to control her horse with her legs or how to use the short bow by talking with Terryn. Kaysie couldn't stop grinning at her friend.

the dark stone keep

Rocks began to jut out of the landscape the second day of their journey to Blackshroud. Purple outlines of mountains were visible over the hills behind the thick pines. Trees grew closer together, and the trail narrowed as it wound up and down the larger rocky hills.

Quynn was beginning to be more aware of how dirty she was. Her long red hair clung to her neck and felt oily, and her hands and legs were brown from the horse. She desperately wanted a bath, but knew the water up here would be pretty cold. Quynn also didn't know how often people really took a bath. From what she had read, there were those who went months without one. Kaysie's short brown hair seemed straighter than usual to Quynn. She knew that it was bothering her friend every time Kaysie messed with her hair. Quynn decided not to say anything.

Kaysie was noticing the rocky outcroppings and the few tall cliffs in the distance. She had seen the mountains in the United States, both the Appalachian and Rocky Mountains. Neither compared to the color, or lack of color, of the rocks in these mountains. They were mostly black. Grays dotted the boulders lying around like a giant had a hissy fit, but they were dark and dull. Kaysie had also seen pictures and TV documentaries of shiny and dull volcanic rock, but those didn't look anything like the ones that were here. It was like they were on an old television show, where everything was in black and white and shades of gray. She felt uneasy as they climbed a particularly tall hill. She wondered how tall a hill could be before it was considered a mountain.

A large stone structure appeared slowly as they crested one of those large, rocky hills. It seemed to be a small castle, like a duke's summer home. Two towers rose above the tall stone walls, connected by an open stone passage. Smaller buildings stood around the towers, though some of the structures were connected by stone and mortar. All the stonework was black. Light did not seem welcome in this place, as the sun's rays seemed devoured by the stones. Kaysie's knees grew weak. Quynn didn't seem too happy to be there, either.

"We're home," Breyah said grimly of the place that Roustin had enslaved her and her sibling

Breyah then closed her eyes, made some complicated hand gestures, and mumbled some strange words under her breath. After a minute of silence, the half-elf opened her eyes and said, "Roustin is not here. There should be no problem getting inside. There is a stable in the back for the horses."

The group rode in complete silence. Kaysie and Quynn kept exchanging glances as their horses picked up speed riding down the steep hill. Both thanked whatever gods were here that they learned to ride as they avoided the black rocks jutting sharply from the landscape and adjusted their weight almost instinctively to avoid falling. Soon, they were in front of the massive wall, stones stacked to at least 30 feet high around the dark forbidding structures. Breyah dismounted and walked to the large wooden arched door and knocked. Kaysie couldn't believe that someone could actually hear through that, but slowly, the door swung open to reveal a tanned half-elven man. Kaysie caught her breath at the sight of the attractive half-elf. His long warm brown hair almost matched his tan and flowed to the middle of his back. His brown eyes reminded her of milk chocolate, his body of a seasoned warrior. She checked herself, turning away and blinking rapidly and trying not to blush. "Yes, sister. You have returned at a good time. I see you have brought Rilee, Quynn, and Kaysie. Come in, quickly," he said looking at all of them in turn.

"Kaysie…Quynn…Rilee—this is Roanallyn, one of my brothers," Terryn said.

"Roan," he said to the group, and smiled and nodded briefly and ushered them in with a sweep of his arms. Kaysie melted.

The group walked their horses to the stone stables in the back of the keep. The wooden doors were thin, but were held together by strong steel. The small stalls were lined with pine shavings, a job that seemed to fall to a stablehand, who did not look of elven heritage at all. In fact, he was much shorter. The old halfling waved and directed the new horses into their own stalls. The wooden walls showed a bit of light through a few cracks in the wooden slats, as they took off the saddles and bridles, but other than that, they worked in almost complete darkness.

Everything seemed so large close up. Neither had been to castles in Great Britain or other parts of Europe, so the real thing, someone actually living in one, took the girls by surprise. The enormity of the square-shaped towers that rose over a hundred feet in the air and were topped by dark conical roofs took their breath away. Quynn recognized the walkway that arched from one tower to the other, and the dark stone building that stretched the length of the towers and rose three more stories from the drawing on the scroll. The ground was a mixture of dark gray cobblestones and wide, odd-shaped swaths of dirt, where the stones had vanished by mysterious means. Quynn wondered aloud how anyone could find their way around such a place. Terryn laughed. "It takes awhile, but when you grow up somewhere, you know every nook and cranny."

Roan, Terryn, and Breyah led Rilee, Kaysie, and Quynn to what seemed to be the back door of the small castle. Everything was black and white, and they were the only colors. Quynn looked around, taking in the strange landscape. Something in the left tower window caught her eye. It looked to be a girl's face outlined in the arched stone window. Quickly, the image disappeared.

Roan opened the large heavy wooden door and ushered everyone inside the long stone building. The small room that the group entered into appeared to be a kitchen. A large wooden table had bowls, iron pots and pans, and an odd wooden utensil sticking out piled beneath it. Cupboards lined the walls, and old tan paint pealed from the edges.

A large fireplace sat next to the door, its embers cold. It reminded Kaysie that she was hungry. Her stomach rumbled at the thought. She took out some dried meat and chewed. "We have to hide you, so this is where you'll be staying," Roan was saying, as he led the group past the kitchen and into a hallway.

There were two staircases, one at each end of the wide stone hallway, and the one they were headed toward looked worse for wear. Quynn didn't like the looks of it. Rilee looked at Kaysie. Kaysie looked back and gave a look of disbelief and worry. It was pretty dark at the end of the stairs. Torches in old copper sconces barely illuminated a small circle of light on the stone walls of the otherwise dark stone corridor. Roan continued down the hall as it took a 45-degree turn and ended with a door. "Right this way, m'ladies," he said, opening the door for the visitors and glancing at Kaysie.

Rilee wandered in first, as the girls hung back. There were three torches burning in sconces, giving the room an eerie red glow. Three beds had been set up along the same stone wall, and a shelf and desk and chair sat opposite. A door stood flush with the left wall. Small sturdy chests with domed tops and inset locks sat at the foot of each bed. "You can put the torches in the next room when you sleep," Breyah said, then added, "They will never go out or make any smoke. They're magical."

It was getting late. The three companions stayed in the stone room while the Moonshades brought them a simple dinner of fruits and rabbit. Kaysie wondered how she'd ever sleep. This dungeon-like place scared her. She wanted to talk to Quynn about it, but didn't want Rilee to overhear or think she was a baby. *I may only be fifteen, but I am not a child,* Kaysie thought stubbornly. Kaysie put on her old t-shirt, the one she was wearing when they disappeared from home and landed in this strange place. Sufficiently covered and sure the two others were already asleep, she silently allowed tears to fall down her cheeks as she slowly fell asleep.

the mysterious figure

Kaysie woke up, afraid to move. She had no idea if it was the middle of the night or after lunch. She also had no idea if Roustin could sense her, like Breyah seemed to be able to sense him. Kaysie momentarily wished her watch glowed in the dark, then wondered if they had changed time zones. She smiled in the pitch-blackness of the room and grabbed her watch. Quietly, she walked over to the other door, where Rilee had put the torches. She was amazed that the door's rusty hinges didn't squeak at all, and she put her arm into the red light. 7:00, it read. She wondered what time they went to bed and if she could wake up Quynn. Out of the corner of her eye, Kaysie thought she saw movement. She froze, wondering what someone would think of her watch if this thing tried to kill her. Slowly, Kaysie turned her eyes to the left. It looked to be a girl in a long black robe. The darkness of her long thick hair blended into the shadow of the garment. Brown eyes glittered in the torchlight. But as soon as Kaysie made eye contact with the girl, she was gone. Heart pounding, Kaysie quietly and quickly closed the door. She made her way back to the bed, covered herself completely with the covers, and stayed there until Quynn awoke.

Kaysie whispered to her friend exactly what happened. "Maybe she's that girl I saw in the window yesterday," Quynn finally said, "Maybe we should tell the others that this place is haunted."

Rilee stirred when the door to the room opened and a torch floated inside followed by Breyah and Terryn holding platters of food. "Breakfast!" Terryn said softly.

The two girls didn't even question the floating torch after all they had been through. It was the first warm food the girls had eaten since leaving Keldon's Hill. It was only thickened vegetable soup, but it tasted like manna from Heaven to Quynn and Kaysie. The girls kept complimenting the Moonshades on their cooking, despite the half-elves' amused smiles. Rilee ate in silence, seeming to be pondering something of great importance. Finally, he asked, "So, who is that girl I keep seeing?"

Kaysie spoke up. "A girl in a black dress with raven-black hair and brown eyes?"

"I did not see her eyes, as she moved too quickly, but yes. I saw her face in a window as we arrived at the castle," Rilee said, surprised at Kaysie's remark.

Breyah and Terryn looked at each other. "That was probably Sevyn," Breyah finally answered, "She knows that we are here. My little sister knows we are running out of time. Sevyn is strong in magic, yet needs more time to learn the proper spells. She is curious, yet shy. Sevyn has a lot of weight on her shoulders."

"Could I meet her?" Quynn asked tentatively, like she was asking to hold a newborn kitten.

The thought of meeting a real wizard, after all she had read, exited the fifteen-year-old. In the back of her mind, she wanted to know if maybe she could learn a few spells.

"I don't see why not," Terryn said.

Kaysie looked nervous. Did she really want to meet the apparition she saw in the next room?

The half-elf in the black robes heard all. Her magic was stronger than anyone thought. She smiled as she thought about how well she hid her powers. Roustin had no idea what was coming. She did sense the nervousness in the two human girls, and she felt both pride and regret in that image. She vowed that she would try and be nice to these two. The half-elf sensed something in the red-haired one, but she couldn't place the feeling. Stepping away from the window, she went to a small thick wooden desk, where a thick leather-bound tome with yellowing pages lay open. She searched its pages of strange symbols until she found the spell she was searching for. The half-elven girl smiled as she memorized the familiar words and gestures that the young mage used to disguise her room from prying eyes.

Quynn and Kaysie wandered up the stairs of the central building, following the directions of Terryn and Breyah. They passed other half-elves that they presumed were other Moonshades. Most looked pleased to see them. One girl looked disappointed. She was pretty small, with long straight blonde hair down to her waist and clear blue eyes. A brother nudged her side, and the girl managed a depressed smile. Quynn stopped. They were on the second floor, and they exited the stairs instead of continuing on to the third floor, where Sevyn was supposed to be. "What's wrong?" Quynn asked the girl seriously.

The little half-elven girl sighed loudly. "I'm Ehirrjirin, thought everyone just calls me Jirin," said the man beside her, "This is Siranasea, my little sister. She's waiting for her 'knight in shining armor' to rescue her. She's upset that girls are coming to her rescue instead."

The half-elven girl shot her brother an annoyed look. Kaysie smiled inwardly that brothers were annoying, no matter where in the world one traveled. She then curtseyed to the two humans. "Siriia," she corrected politely, though shot her brother another look, "It is an honor to finally meet you."

Quynn tried not to smile. "The honor is mine, Siriia. And I am sorry I am not a man here to rescue you."

"That cannot be helped. All that matters is that we will be rid of this dismal place soon," said the young half-elf.

"We should be going," Kaysie spoke up, "We have to see Sevyn."

An older half elven woman, who was scrubbing down the cobblestone floor, looked up and smiled at the girls. Although dressed primarily in brown leathers, hints of green showed through on her shirt under a leather vest and in her jewelry. "I'm Systiri, but call me Jaide," she said, "I trust you have met us all, except for the youngest."

Kaysie nodded. "Just Sevyn."

Jaide scrubbed at a stain on the floor for a moment before adding, "The Arts have left Sevraiean a bit, hmmm, chaotic in her thoughts. Do not take her whims too seriously."

They smiled and nodded at the odd warning, then continued up the stairs to the final floor of the central dark stone building. They saw that the stairs continued up and ended in a doorway to the balcony above. They had seen from the outside that it connected the two towers. Quynn could see the second door on the right that Terryn said was Sevyn's room. Nervously, she made her way to the door. Kaysie was getting that feeling in the pit of her stomach again, but she tried to ignore it. This was it. This was Sevyn.

Sevyn

Quynn and Kaysie looked at each other. "Should I knock?" Quynn whispered.

Kaysie shrugged. "I guess."

As her closed fist was coming down upon the thick wood, the door slowly opened. Kaysie momentarily thought again about those old horror movies, where the door opens by itself to reveal a vampire or a mummy or worse. She didn't realize that her eyes were tightly closed until she opened them again. The door hadn't opened on its own. What she saw surprised her. It was a small half-elven girl, maybe five feet tall, in long, dark robes. The cloth surrounding the half-elf had silver embroidery stitched carefully into it that looked to be ancient writing around the sleeves, and the hem dragged the floor. Long wavy thick ebony hair seemed to flow into the design of the robe, flowing free around her shoulders like a dark waterfall. Brown eyes told of a long, hard life, though she looked so young. "Sevyn."

It was a statement, not a question, from Kaysie. "Kaysie," she said in an alto voice that almost seemed too deep for her, yet just perfect somehow, "Quynn. Come inside."

The two girls wordlessly followed the waif into a good-sized square-shaped stone room. It seemed to double as a bedroom and study, as a large arched window let sunlight flow directly onto a tall, square table, just big enough for the large leather-bound book open to a page only Sevyn could understand. A large empire canopy bed sat in the back corner of the room, the headboard against the wall, curtains of a thin black fabric draped over the poles. Everything seemed so big for this tiny half-elf. "Nice to finally meet you in person," she said to Kaysie.

Kaysie shivered involuntarily. This Sevyn made her nervous, like she knew infinitely more than she let on. Quynn looked a bit uncomfortable, but seemed to know more what to expect. "You, too," Quynn answered calmly, "Lovely room."

"Thank you. Roustin helped out a little," she smiled to herself at that last comment.

"You have figured a way out of here, and possibly bring us home?" Quynn continued, after a brief uncomfortable pause and after she realized Kaysie wasn't going to say anything.

"Yes," said Sevyn, after a moment, turning from her guests and sitting down upon a high-backed wooden chair that sat before the desk.

She motioned for Kaysie and Quynn to pull up two other chairs. Sevyn noticed immediately that she made Kaysie nervous. The half-elf was amused. "I have been working on several spells. They need more work, and my siblings protest that I need more protection. They seem to think that you two will bide time for me to get us all out of here."

Blunt, but to the point, Quynn thought, I like her. Sevyn continued. "I also think you were sent here by some other force, knowing that we were here. I have not figured this one out yet."

Kaysie thought about it. Was that how Carry knew about the scroll? Did she know about the Moonshades and Roustin? Was she trying to warn them of the danger or prevent them from coming? She wanted to ask Quynn what she thought, but didn't want to leave Sevyn out of the conversation. Kaysie fidgeted in her chair. "Yes?" Sevyn asked, turning to Kaysie, "Is there something you have discovered?"

"Uh, um, er, um, uh…" she stammered, then turned her head, not really wanting to speak.

"I don't bite," Sevyn said with a trace of sarcasm.

Quynn tried not to stare as she thought that Sevyn looked like a small child, and she just might be in half-elven years. Kaysie continued to talk to the stone floor, tracing the creases with her leather booted foot. "The woman who was trying to stop us. I was trying to figure out if she was trying to warn us of the danger or trying to stop us from rescuing you and your siblings."

Sevyn looked at Kaysie intently. "Woman? Hmm. Had she acted strangely before this?"

Kaysie nodded without stopping to think. She remembered quite well the bizarre behavior of Carry with the old tack room. "Ah-hmm. I must ask you to leave, as I want to study something a bit more," the half-elf said pensively.

Sevyn smiled as the two girls walked out of the room, politely waving to their backs. "Maybe I can get some work done, now that they have met me," Sevyn mumbled to herself.

With that, she closed the heavy wooden door with little effort and went back to the large tomes.

the wizard is home

Quynn and Kaysie were about to wander back down, when they heard footsteps running up the stairs. Breyah rounded the corner like a galloping horse toward the bewildered girls. Instantly, both of them felt the tension in the hallway. Kaysie's heart began to pound. "You must return to your room quickly! Roustin is on his way back!" Breyah exclaimed, breathless, "And you two are not armed with sword or sorcery!"

Like lightning, Breyah led the girls back down the steps to their room in the dungeons, as Quynn and Kaysie were beginning to call it. The wolf ran at their heals, panting, oblivious to the danger. They noticed the other Moonshades scrambling around the castle, straightening rugs, dusting off statues and trinkets, and fluffing pillows. There was no time for questions. Soon, Quynn and Kaysie were plunged into the near darkness, into the waning light of the stone walled "dungeons."

Breyah had run back upstairs, leaving them with the warning of not to move. She had nothing to worry about. The two girls sat on the back corner bed, clutching at each other like scared toddlers. As unreligious as Kaysie was, she wanted to pray to whatever gods or goddesses were out there to protect them. She had no idea the true power a necromancer had, or what this one was capable of. Kaysie wanted to ask her best friend all she knew, but was afraid to speak, even though Breyah said nothing about whispering.

Quynn realized her eyes were tightly shut when she saw the orange-red glow of the torch light from the inside of her eyelids. She wanted to know what was going on, how she could help, when Sevyn would be ready. The only idea she had about the time it took to prepare spells came from her books. Quynn didn't know if that applied to real life. Quynn was also afraid to speak, though she knew if Roustin could magically sense their presence like Breyah could sense his, that speaking wouldn't harm their chances any. "We've got to be brave," Quynn whispered, more for herself than for Kaysie.

Kaysie nodded, shaking like a sapling in a bad thunderstorm. "What can we do? I hate just sitting here, not knowing. Roustin will know if we're here, if he has the same powers as Breyah. What powers does a necromancer have, anyway?"

"Well," Quynn began, thinking out loud about the powers of mages from her books, "I could rattle off a few schools of magic from my fantasy books, but it probably wouldn't make any sense to you. Anyway, I'm not even sure what he can't use, unless of course, he's got a scroll, like the one that brought us here. Wizards can use any spell they want if it's on a scroll. But, I guess spells that have to do with death and raising the dead, mostly."

That didn't have the desired effect for Kaysie, which was to make her feel better, knowing certain things he couldn't do to her. She did laugh, though it was out of nervousness. "You were supposed to make me feel better," she voiced to her best friend, trying to sound annoyed, but smiling anyway.

Quynn smiled in the eerie red light that mingled with the dark shadows. "Sorry," she said, "Necromancers are rather powerful. Too bad we don't have anything to counter him with."

Kaysie got a mischievous look on her face, though it was hard for Quynn to tell in the dim torchlight. Kaysie's voice gave away her feelings. "We haven't yet looked around this dungeon. Maybe there's something that would work, at least until Sevyn is ready."

Quynn returned the grin. "Let's start the dungeon crawl," falling upon jargon used in her fantasy games.

After all the books Quynn had read, she wanted to check for traps on every door, search for hidden doors and spaces behind the walls, and find random gold pieces in corners if she looked hard enough. She had a feeling, though, that it might not be nearly as exciting and that she and Kaysie would find more dust and long forgotten trash than gold and jewels. The room was still lit with a few of the magical torches, the flame hovering over the sconces, giving the room an eerie red glow. Kaysie went to the left, and Quynn went right along the wall. The room beside theirs through the side door was bigger than either had previously thought. It was also a weird shape; Nevada, crossed Quynn's mind, without the point at the bottom. It was piled high with boxes on top of low shelves and a few tall wardrobes. They started with the shelves. Books and papers lined the dark wooden structures, gathering layers dust. Kaysie coughed and remarked, "It's like we're cleaning the tack room all over again, except this is so much bigger."

Quynn managed a smile. She was half expecting to find another scroll wrapped in a long leather scrap. "Hey, Quynn," Kaysie called from the opposite wall after a few minutes of searching, "Come look at these."

In her hand was a pile of small, beaten steel points in a small wooden box. "Arrowheads," the girls said at the same time, exchanging a quick glance. Kaysie was thrilled to have discovered something rather useful.

"Can you put these on arrow shafts?" Quynn asked her friend, smiling.

"I can put a shoe on a horse," Kaysie replied, "That's my only skill in metalwork, that I know of."

Kaysie deposited the small box in one of the pouches Rilee had given them. After some more searching and discovering only a few dead spiders and a lot of abandoned junk, Quynn suddenly broke the silence. "Take a look at these pictures."

"We don't have time for that, Quynn. Look for something we can use. We can find something that matches your room back home later." Kaysie sounded preoccupied and a bit annoyed.

"Excuse me, this is important," Quynn retorted, "These are like the scroll that brought us here, except the drawings are different."

Kaysie sighed and walked over to her best friend, thinking that this would probably be a waste of time. But when she saw the detail of the drawings on the old parchment and the intricate words that surrounded them like the letters were actually vines, she gasped. These made the drawing of the tower look like a small child crayoned it. The detail that the scribe used with nothing but ink was practically photorealistic. Quynn showed her friend pictures of a wizard hurling a ball of fire bigger than the page, the wizard shimmering behind it, and of a transparent hand surrounded by mists like the genies of legend. "I have an idea of what these spells might be," Quynn said, "If we are indeed in my books."

The boxes were harder to explore. Most couldn't be opened, just using their hands as levers. The ones they could open contained forests of sawdust covering weapons, armor, and clothes. It was actually the clothes that got them the most excited. A box revealed cloth shirts in several colors and a few with thin leather strings that laced up the shirt, part way down. Although they were tempted to put those on, they were too big, so they opted for a short-sleeved cloth shirt that hung loosely off their shoulders. Quynn grabbed for a dark forest green shirt, and Kaysie picked out a dark brown one to match her pants. After returning to their room through the secret door to change into their new-found clothes, they continued their search.

Quynn and Kaysie also took two ornate short swords that they had seen their new friends use, and a short bow that was intricately carved, then went back into their room to change into their pants and new shirts. The girls hoped that this small arsenal would be enough.

another presence at Blackshroud Castle

The wizard felt that there were two new creatures in his keep. It confused him. Concentrating, he tried to decipher what they were. Humanoid, if not humans, he decided. Female. The wizard tried to discover their abilities, but could not get past his own magical barriers. He decided not to force it, though he could break them at a thought. The mage did not feel like wasting the time it would take to rebuild the magic. The wizard ceased thinking of it as his horse began to stray from the well-worn trail.

The horse and master looked to be made out of only black and white and millions of shades of gray, out of place on the green hill and under the cloudless blue sky. Only the mysterious runes magically stitched into the dark gray robes of the wizard seemed to reflect the sun's rays. The wizard startled his black stallion into a brisk trot. The horse's neck came up suddenly as he moved toward the keep. Two black tails seemed to flow from the stallion's back; one made of long thick obsidian-colored strands of hair, the other from dark shadowed cloth and silvery magical runes.

As the black stone keep came into view, the wizard tried again. This time, the presence felt stronger. There was an urgency in his need to know what powers these new beings had. He slowed his horse. Concentrating once again, the image of two female humans came into his vision. One was pretty strong. Warrior of some sort, he decided, seeing a short sword hanging from a scabbard at her waist. The other was more difficult. There was an aura surrounding her that he knew all too well, yet he didn't want to admit the power of it.

69

This barrier made it hard to be sure, though he knew in his black heart what it must be. Another wizard. A powerful one. But there were no adornments, no pouches with the required material components for spells that most needed to work. She must be powerful indeed, to have no need for spell components, the wizard decided. *This will be quite a battle,* he thought, *I could use the challenge.* The wizard smiled an evil, devilish grin that made his dark eyes look like bottomless black holes during this sun-drenched day.

battle lines

"We're armed now," Kaysie proclaimed when the surprised half elves saw the two humans coming in from around the corner.

The Moonshades were pleased to see Quynn and Kaysie armed to the teeth and ready to help. The two girls had waltzed upstairs to discover the siblings huddled around each other inside a room that looked to be a lavish study, speaking in low tones. Kaysie noticed that Sevyn wasn't among them and whispered it to Quynn. Kaysie had her bow in hand, a quiver of arrows slung over a shoulder. A short sword hung loosely off her hip from a hangar that slipped smoothly onto her black leather belt. Quynn had rolled up all the scrolls together and had put them in her backpack, though she also had her bow in hand and a quiver over her shoulder.

A small, thin wisp of a figure seemed to float over the stone floor and through the open doorway. The dark cloak stitched with silver runes barely gave the girl depth, and a ratty leather belt looped around the tiny waist, pouches loosely hanging from thick leather cords filled with strange-smelling substances tugging the belt towards the ground. Tiny soft-soled boots made almost no sound across the stone floor as they carried the figure toward Quynn and Kaysie. "I am ready," said a familiar soft low female voice.

Sevyn smiled, and light hit her mouth, full of bright white teeth and a lot of mischief. Her older siblings looked a bit mystified and a bit scared, but nodded. Quynn and Kaysie looked back and forth between the groups, looking for a hint as to what to do next. "We all have talents," Jaide spoke up after a pause, "Magic, divine and from

71

within, and different fighting abilities. Those with arrows, the real kind and the magical kind, need to use them from the windows. You're our first line of defense. Once the rest of us get in close, stop shooting and start in with your other abilities or weapons. Please don't shoot me with an arrow!"

Her light humor got a nervous laugh. No one was looking forward to this battle, though getting out was on the top of everyone's mind.

"Allow me, before you engage Roustin in combat."

A condescending voice from the back spoke up, low and with carefully chosen words. "You will never stand a chance against someone like him. You should know that."

Sevyn walked around the group, looking at them all in turn. "There are reasons he doesn't suspect me. I have my ways. Let me weaken him first. Then, you can have him."

She stopped, turning to look at the group expectantly, like a teacher seeing if the class understood her instructions. "Sev," Roan began, almost in a pleading tone, "I know you're strong; we know you're strong. But you can't take on Roustin yet."

The ends of the small half-elf's mouth went up at the corners, taking her deep brown eyes with them. They reflected an inner fire that Quynn and Kaysie had not seen in their earlier encounter with the young wizard. Her eyes wanted to laugh, but not at something funny, but at ignorance that only they knew. "You should know me better than that, my brother. Leave me to my own talents, and I shall leave you to yours."

Roan shook his head. "You have always been stubborn. Yes, you may have your way this once, but we shall have your back."

Kaysie knew it was the end of the conversation by his tone. Her mother used it all the time. The two humans looked at each other out of the corner of their eyes as if to try and reassure each other.

The wizard read through a thick, heavy tome covered in thick leather and bound together with a sturdy iron lock. The key lay in a pocket amongst the folds of the gray robe that fit around the strong body loosely. His stallion stood nearby, tied to a tree and tearing at the grass as he ate. A few travelers wandering the well-worn path did not notice this scene before them. Roustin would look up occasionally and smile to himself. How he loved magic. Engaging once more in his book, the wizard slowly memorized the passages, going over and over the familiar incantations and gestures until he knew he could once again repeat the spells. This new presence in the towers disturbed him. He wanted to be prepared. Soon, the tome was slid carefully back into its case and was slung over the stallion. His hood drawn, it seemed Death himself was riding toward Blackshroud Castle.

The tall wooden double doors loomed up over the last hill as the dark stone walls became visible. One was slightly open, an inconsistency that Roustin knew not everyone would notice. This wizard knows I'm here, the necromancer thought. His fingers did a small dance and traced patterns only he could see, and his mouth formed words only a few knew, then, he stopped before the incantation was completed. Concentrating, the wizard knew he could keep this until he needed it, at least until he knew what was peeking at him from the door. Soon, Roustin knew, and he let the spell fade from his mind. It was his apprentice, that little half-elf, the seventh in her family of slaves. He smiled at the thought, though erased it quickly as he approached the door. He yawned quite suddenly, confused at this strange action, as he dismounted. Sevyn opened the wide door for the old wizard. "Tired, Master?" Sevyn innocently said, taking the reins of his horse.

"I don't know what came over me," Roustin said without thinking, then stiffly, "It was a long ride."

Sevyn allowed Roustin to walk in front of her as she led the horse to the stables. She nodded once, then twice. Suddenly, there was a dark figure between Sevyn and Roustin. Just as suddenly, the figure was gone. Sevyn noticed that a few of the small pouches that hung around the wizard's waist were now oddly shaped. She smiled to herself. Soon, the horse was put into the old halfling's hands, and the two wizards made their way back to the towers.

eavesdropping…

The two wizards walked into the kitchen, the first room that Quynn and Kaysie had seen in this old castle. Jaide was busy ladling the necromancer's supper of thin soup with unevenly cut vegetables and small chunks of gray meat into a small bowl. Sevyn stood by the table as the old wizard sat on the graying wooden bench by the stove. The table was thick and tall, but like the bench that matched it in age and color, it was cracking with neglect. Jaide avoided eye contact with her master as she carefully set the bowl in front of him. She stood again, silent. "What is this?" he snapped, eyeing the food before him, "I save your mother, and this is the food I get? This carrion is not fit for the wolves!"

Sevyn stiffened and kept her eyes on the cobblestones below her feet. Jaide shot a quick glance at her youngest sister, a warning of silence. Jaide said nothing, then focused on the cobblestone floor beneath her feet. "Ah, no answer, eh? Just for that, there will be no supper for you," the wizard snapped.

He glared at Jaide, his piercing dark eyes threatening to bore holes in the half-elf. She said nothing. The bench screeched against the stone floor as he stood slowly, trying to hide his weakening joints, "Bring me something edible in my study! Sevraiean," he added calmly, "You will bring me my food."

The wizard glared at Jaide as if she were a cockroach. He stalked off, slamming the door behind him, leaving the half-elves in his wake. Sevyn didn't move. She was used to his treatment, though he did not use her full name often. Jaide stood for a moment like a statue, then,

74

turned to remake her master's dinner.

Quynn, Kaysie, and Rilee heard Roustin screaming from the lavish study. They waited until the footsteps had gone before whispering. "I'm quieter than you, um, at the moment, anyway," Quynn glanced down at Kaysie's arsenal, "I'll follow him to see what he's up to."

"Be careful," said Kaysie with a hint of nervousness that she tried to hide behind a small cough.

"I'll go check on Jaide," Rilee said, sounding concerned, "I want to make sure she's ok."

He softly stepped out of the room, hardly making a sound on the cobblestones of the floor with his leather shoes. The two girls shrugged. Kaysie got down on her knees, to better hide behind a large overstuffed red chair. She decided to ready her bow, in case she needed it. Tall built-in bookshelves lined the wall to her right. Kaysie tried not to lean on the dusty fraying covers as she waved to Quynn. There was no door, only an arched stone opening into the hall beyond, so Kaysie watched her friend disappear around the corner.

Quynn made it to the stairs when she heard the kitchen door close with a small thud and then, the sound of soft leather soles against stone. Quickly, she hid behind a large dark wood cabinet, crouching in the darkness. She couldn't see, but Quynn could hear the soft, deliberate footfalls. Sevyn, Quynn guessed, thinking of the younger half-elf bringing the haughty mage his evening meal. The footfalls faded into the darkness of the second floor. Quynn quickly and quietly emerged from hiding and followed. Soon, she, too, was enveloped into the growing shadows of twilight.

Kaysie sat cramped behind the chair, every sound making her jump, hands shaking. She tried to slow her breathing, but the breaths were shaking as much as her hands. *Get a hold of yourself,* she wanted to scream. *Just because I'm in a dark castle with wizards and shadows and spirits—* she thought of Sevyn's apparition—*doesn't mean I should be this jumpy.* Kaysie tried to concentrate on her bow lessons.

She pretended to aim and shoot, then took out the arrowheads she had found. Kaysie sat, trying to figure out how they attached to the arrow shaft. Lost in thought, Kaysie patiently took a shaft from her quiver and tried to tie the head onto it. It fell, sideways. Not wanting to admit defeat, Kaysie started to try again, but heard movement. She froze, trying to figure out if it was her imagination, or if she needed to ready her weapon. The footsteps drew closer.

Kaysie quietly drew a fresh arrow and nocked it in place. She crouched behind the chair, bent at a few funny angles, but she still attempted to aim at the approaching figure. Kaysie strained to hear the hushed voices, but it was like hearing a conversation through a mound of feathers. Kaysie thought about trying to shoot two arrows at once, like Quynn had told her about in her books back home, but decided not to chance it. Suddenly, the footsteps stopped. Kaysie hoped that whoever it was had not noticed her. Then, a soft sound of metal against leather hit Kaysie's ears. It didn't take long for her to comprehend the sound—a sword coming out of a scabbard. She readied her bow and arrow, ready to shoot at whoever moved into her view. The footsteps started again. Kaysie stood, as best she could behind the chair, feeling it move against her weight. She cringed inwardly at the grinding, but managed to still herself. The footsteps became more deliberate, like the owner didn't care any longer if someone heard them. Kaysie stood tall and straight and pulled back the bowstring. A male figure appeared in the doorway. The arrow flew straight at him. The figure tried to duck, but wasn't fast enough. The point of the arrow stuck in a thick belt pouch, held together with leather and wood and varnished in a black dye. The figure gasped, then, put both hands on the hilt of the long sword. Kaysie noticed her error first. "Stop! Aren't you Jirin?"

She backed up against the bookcase, in case her warning was too late. The steel blade stopped inches from her hand. A shorter figure came around the corner and tilted her head sideways to get a better look. Long sandy colored hair flowed past her waist. "Siriia?"

"Kaysie?" they both said.

Then, Jirin sheathed his sword and lowered his head. "I am so sorry that I just tried to kill you."

Kaysie tried not to smile at his gallant apology. "It's ok. I am fine. I almost got you with that arrow. Are you alright?"

"I'm fine, but I am not so sure of my pouch," he said smiling, then weakly, "You're a good shot."

"You're good at stopping your sword," Kaysie answered, allowing herself to smile again, now that her breathing was back to normal.

"We need to get going, brother," Siriia said irritably, "Sevyn can't hold him off forever."

Kaysie noticed a twinge of jealousy in her voice as Siriia spoke of her youngest sister. "Come with us," Jirin said smiling, "And I promise I won't try to kill you again."

mage-speak

Quynn rounded the stairs as silently as a cat stalking its prey. She kept Sevyn just barely in her sight in the twilight shadows that were coming in through the small windows. If the half-elf noticed the human following, she made no move to stop her. Sevyn slowly made her way past all three floors in the central building between the two towers, carefully holding Roustin's soup on a small wooden tray. The stairs continued to ascend to a thick wooden door ornately carved with abstract designs that appeared to be anguished faces in the right light. Quynn decided that this was the right light and shuddered at the grotesque and haunting images. Sevyn leaned against the right wall, the tray balancing on her small hip, and turned the large copper knob. Trapped door, Quynn thought to herself, ducking in time for an arrow to fly out of a small opening beside the door at head level, missing her by inches. It landed harmlessly in the soft mortar of the wall inbetween two worn stones. Quynn let out a breath she didn't know she was holding, then stilled herself. If Sevyn noticed, she didn't let on.

The half-elf then disappeared around the door, but didn't close it. Quynn wondered if Sevyn knew she was following her. She then wondered if closing the door reset the arrow trap. After a few seconds, Quynn silently followed the small girl through the door and was met with a soft cool breeze. Outside... She emerged onto a stone walkway with high stone walls on each side, the stone rising at a steep slope as it drew nearer to doors on either end. The moonlight illuminated part of the walkway, sending straight shadows towards the doors.

Quynn noticed the door on the left slowly closing and walked towards that one. She noticed the walkway led to the two towers as she reached the left door. The carvings on this one seemed identical to the one she just passed through, but for one major difference: the faces seemed to be unique, with different intricacies in their expressions, like these weren't carvings at all. Quynn swallowed her fear and stepped through the door.

A wide staircase was to her right, winding up the square room like it was really a circle. A dais stood in front of Quynn. The two stone steps led up to a great empire canopy bed. The legs and frame seemed carved from the floor as the stone reached for the high ceiling. Thick and sheer drapery of all shades of gray wrapped over the tall posts of the bed. Candles sat on low shelves around the room, their wicks blackened with soot and ash, and the wax frozen into long thick droplets. Ornate long bladed daggers hung on the wall, crossed like a knight's sword in leather and steel sheaths. Many corked ceramic pots and jars filled the shelves alongside several thick books bound with intricate locks. The stoppered jars still permeated powerful smells into the room, giving everything an overbearing stench. Quynn shuddered. She couldn't explain why, but she swore the lavishly decorated bedroom smelled of death. Quynn wondered if this room was Roustin's. The stone was of the same black and gray stone that seemed to have all its color drained from it by evil means.

Quynn heard voices from above, from the direction of the stairs. Silently, she crept next to the wall up the stairs, climbed halfway to the next floor, stopped, and listened. "Here is your dinner, m'lord," Quynn heard Sevyn's low, soft voice say, then heard the sound of the tray being set upon a table.

Roustin mumbled something that Quynn couldn't comprehend. She shifted, lifting herself over two steps, straining to hear the conversation. There was a shuffling. Quynn wondered what was going on. Then, there was a crackling noise; a fire in the fireplace, Quynn thought. Chairs grinded across the stone floor. "I don't know why I treat you so well, giving you a nice room and letting you learn the arts from me," Roustin's haughty voice came from beyond the stairs, "You are just as worthless as your siblings."

The remark was met with silence from Sevyn.

"You are slow when it comes to magic. I do not think that you have the inner spark of a mage. Your potions are nothing but colored water." Roustin's voice sounded haughty, like he was trying to convince himself of his own words.

Quynn waited, unmoving, for a smart retort from Sevyn, but was her patience was rewarded with more silence.

"I am wasting my time with you," Roustin slammed something on a wooden table, a mug, Quynn guessed, then heard a dull thud like a swift clap. Quynn startled at the sound.

"Leave me to choke down this pig slop that your useless sister has prepared," Roustin snapped

Quynn was trying to comprehend what just happened when she suddenly realized that Sevyn was walking towards her. Quickly and quietly, Quynn retraced her steps to the door, hurried outside, and ran towards the door leading to the central building. She remembered not to shut it as she jogged back to the study where she left her best friend behind an overstuffed chair.

missing—

Quynn ran back to the room where she had left her best friend to discover that Kaysie was gone. Quynn's mind raced, forgetting the scene that she had left. Did Kaysie tell her she would go anywhere? Did anyone need her best friend's help with anything? Quynn heard a noise, like leather sliding across stone. Footsteps. Quynn quickly ducked behind the chair and waited. She crouched, perfectly still, straining to hear where the noises were coming from, and maybe, where they were going. The sound was getting louder, coming toward the room where Quynn was hiding. She tried to blend into the bookcase as two figures came into the room. Quynn watched Jaide and Rilee appear from around the stone archway and come into the room. She let out a sigh of relief. "Where's Kaysie?" Quynn looked from one to the other, both friends giving her a blank expression.

Jaide shrugged. "I haven't seen her."

"I told her to stay here, but obviously she didn't." Quynn's voice sounded concerned, rather than angry, as she looked around the room, as if Kaysie would appear from behind a secret door in the bookcase.

"We have to find her," Rilee said matter-of-factly, "But be careful. And be quiet."

Quynn told them briefly what she had heard while crouched on the stairway from the room in the tower. Jaide nodded, then said, "Roustin is not there now. I was in the tower for a little while, and it was deserted."

The group went back into the long hallway, wary of every shadow. The full moon's rays made long black monsters out of the sparse furniture dotting the hallway. Quynn searched for her best friend in rooms she had never been in, rooms filled with statues of strange creatures, high dark wooden tables, and thick tomes. With every dark corner and every black shadow, her fear grew. It was the stone figure in the atrium that caught Quynn's attention.

In the center of the foyer stood a statue of a wizard. The elaborate thick necklace with a large gemstone pendant hanging at his chest oddly wasn't carved like the rest, as if the statue was a large elaborate hook. The man was dressed in long robes, flowing in an imagined breeze. In his left arm, the statue cradled a thick book and held a long straight stone wand in the other hand, beard flying in the same imagined wind that seemed to fill the grand front entrance. The sculpture sat on a tall rune-carved pedestal, appearing to be carved out of the floor below. Rilee shuddered and glanced at Jaide. "Wasn't he a tale to frighten children?"

Jaide shook her head. "Dargontus Kelrune was real."

Quynn stared at the incredible detail of this statue, barely hearing the conversation going on beside her. Dargontus. The name sounded familiar to her. "Who was this Dargontus?" Quynn asked, trying to recall her books and hoping Jaide would fill in what she could not remember.

Jaide looked at Quynn as if she just sprouted antennae and proclaimed herself a centaur. "A mage," the half-elf barely got out, then corrected herself, "An archmage. It is the highest title given to wizards. Some say he learned the secret of immortality and that he put his life force in that amulet around his neck, just in case his body should not last through the experiments. No one really knows what ever became of him. Anyway, Kaysie isn't here, so we'd better look elsewhere."

With that, Jaide turned to go through a door to her left. Quynn began to remember the stories of the powerful archmage, the necromancer Dargontus, from her fantasy novels. She could not remember the story, either, even with Jaide's little bit of information. As she thought about it, though, Quynn realized that Rilee and Jaide had moved on to the next room, so she followed quickly behind her new friends. It was a small room that she entered into through the heavy wood door. It looked to be a small gathering area, a place to entertain guests. A few chairs, a table, and a few cabinets covered in a rather thick layer of dust sat close together, leaving little room to move. Quynn decided not to think about Roustin's lack of social skills, just in case he could read minds, too. "Not here," Rilee said, stating the obvious.

"Upstairs," Jaide announced, and they all followed, figuring she knew the best places to look.

Upon reaching the top of the stairs, Quynn held out an arm to signal for her friends to stop and listen. For a few seconds, the only sounds were of three people breathing and a few squeaks and groans of the keep. Then, she heard it again; a low laugh and a few unintelligible words, the sounds rising and falling like some arcane song. "Well, it's not Kaysie," Jaide whispered.

"Sevyn?" Rilee raised an eyebrow.

Jaide nodded. "She has begun her spells." Quynn couldn't decipher Jaide's emotions.

They went a little faster up the wide staircase, the sounds getting louder. Quynn was both scared and excited as she followed her two new friends.

the magical song

The sound grew louder as the group ran upstairs as fast as they could. Down the hallway to the left, a sickly yellow light fell upon the floor, shifting erratically, illuminating the once dark hallway from Sevyn's room. A tall shadow obscured part of the light, making the edges of the figure glow unnaturally. Quynn recognized Kaysie's form and started to run forward, her mouth beginning to form her best friend's name, but Rilee held her firmly with a strong hand on her shoulder. "There's a dangerous spell in progress," he said firmly, "I wouldn't interrupt it, m'lady."

Quynn looked up at her friend, then sighed in resignation. Deep down, she knew Rilee was right. She hoped Kaysie was okay in that trance-like state in front of the door. Jaide looked at Rilee curiously. "What do you know of magic?"

"I know a few tricks here and there," he answered, reddening in the magical light.

"Oh?" Jaide asked, as the magical light grew in intensity, then changed to a sickly green.

Rilee hesitated. "Uh, well, I get my abilities from The Goddess, Feiwya."

The color spread to his ears, reminding Quynn of when she stayed on the phone too long. "A warrior of the forest, as I have long suspected." Jaide smiled.

"For several years," Rilee said modestly, as the light again grew in intensity, then switched to a deathly pale blue.

Quynn tuned out their conversation as she began to rack her brain. *What would I do in my role-playing games if my character were in this predicament?* "We can't just stand here, cowering like, well, cowards, until we all blow up!" Quynn exploded suddenly, as Jaide and Rilee looked at her, mouths slightly open, "We have to do something! We don't know what's going on in there, yes, but we need to find out! Rilee, you said you knew a bit of magic. Get as close as you can to Kaysie and see what's going on. I'm going to search for the rest of the Moonshades."

With that, Quynn stormed off down the hallway, staying as close as she could to the balcony overlooking the large statue downstairs, scanning for the rest of the half-elves.

Rilee seemed to meld with the shadows as he made his way towards Kaysie. She stayed completely still as he reached the human girl. The words of magic became louder. The colored lights began to change more rapidly, as if stained glass were being held in front of a flame. The spell was reaching a fevered pitch. Rilee paused inside the first doorway. Kaysie's straight brown hair fanned at the edges in the still air. Her clothes rustled as if in a light summer breeze. Another cadence was reached in the magical song. Rilee moved forward, just barely paying attention to his footfalls. When he was close enough to Kaysie that he could reach out and touch her, Rilee got his first look inside Sevyn's room. An intricate pattern was etched into the stone floor, the grooves glowing a deathly green-yellow. A small figure with her back to the young warrior stood in the center, arms outstretched, chanting words that Rilee didn't understand. Her long black hair swirled in the magical wind. An oval made of wood carved with intricate runes that seemed to have grown into a stand that looked like roots from a tree stood on the far edge of the carved circle. The center glowed brightly, colors changing every few seconds, from that sickly yellow to pale green to a frost-bitten blue, swirling, then back again in a pattern known only to its creator. Thick books lay strewn over a large table, pages marked with ribbon and colored leather swaths. The brass locks on some of the books glowed eerily in the otherwise dark room. Rilee noticed that some of the locks seemed to have no place for a key or a combination. His magic knew of no such spells for opening them, though it seemed an easy task for Sevyn. Just as he was going to turn and go back to Jaide and, probably, Quynn, Rilee felt a cold skeleton-like hand on his shoulder. He let his eyes fall upon a long coarse black sleeve, just beyond a shoulder, and finally to a lined, ashen face. Roustin Blackfyre.

reaching a cadence in the magical song

Rilee had just formulated "Roustin" in his brain along with a few words that he would not say in the presence of ladies when a burning sensation coursed through his body. Quynn saw her friend shake violently as tiny yellow bolts darted around Roustin's hand, then, in seconds had writhed to surround Rilee. His mouth opened and closed, then, lay still. Suddenly, she saw the whites of Rilee's eyes. Roustin held up the limp body like a child trying to get a rag doll to walk.

Quynn instinctively drew her bow and fired a metal-tipped arrow in a single fluid motion that flew straight and true. Roustin raised an eyebrow at the sound of the moving air. Suddenly, the missile swerved and plunked deep in the mortar behind him. Jaide raised her arm in front of Quynn. "That won't work," the oldest Moonshade sibling whispered, keeping both eyes on the mage, "He is immune to weapons that are not magically enhanced."

"And how did you find that one out?" Roustin sneered, mockingly, letting Rilee's body fall to the floor in an unceremonious heap and advancing on the two women.

Sevyn's chants drowned out Roustin's footfalls. Cadences rose and fell over the advancing mage. Jaide was silent, but she unblinkingly kept her eyes trained on the necromancer. "Where are my parents, you bastard?" she spat, brimming with venom.

Quynn startled a little behind the half-elf. She had never seen Jaide allow anger to overcome her. Quynn decided to keep silent, greatly worried about her friend, who was lying helplessly on the cold stone floor. She wanted to think of something to do, something to save her best friend, her new friends, and poor Rilee—was he—Quynn choked a little on the thought, then dismissed it quickly from her mind. Maybe Roustin wouldn't notice her. No, there was too much light coming from Sevyn's room, even with Kaysie's body now swaying in the middle of the doorway to the rhythm of the magical song.

"Ooo," Roustin looked at Jaide in mock surprise, "Those words should not cross a lady's lips." Showing both hands, he continued, "I do not have your parents."

Quynn took that moment to try again. Safely in the corner of the hallway, she aimed and fired again, in one perfect fluid motion, a talent that she didn't know she had. It flew unwavering toward the mage and buried itself in his shoulder. A small circle of blood soaked through onto the dark cloak; then, the arrow fell to the ground in with a sharp clatter of wood on stone. The mage hardly noticed the arrow, but he noticed Quynn. "I told you that wouldn't work, Quynn!" Jaide practically hissed, still not taking her eyes off of Roustin, even to blink.

Kaysie took that moment to start mumbling unintelligibly along with Sevyn. Their voices rose and fell together, as if possessed by an unseen force. Roustin turned, just for a second. Jaide pounced, like a lioness waiting for her prey to stumble. She had him pinned to the ground, her knees digging into his thighs, one hand on his arm, the other drawing an ornate dagger from a hidden wrist sheath, a long thin blade that glinted eerily in the glow of magic. In a moment of clarity, Quynn screamed, "No! Jaide! Don't you see? Roustin is the only one who knows how to find your parents! You'll never find them without this mage!"

Suddenly, Quynn wished she had kept her mouth shut. Roustin had them just where he wanted. Unknowingly, she had given the mage a chance to live.

silence...

Visions of pain, betrayal, death, destruction, red, red, blood. Then, darkness. All senses were deadened. A woman touched an arm in surprise. Someone else might be there with her in this void. Kaysie felt the touch in the darkness of the long slender fingers, yet didn't know why she did not have the will to respond.

Sevyn felt the cold rounded stones of the floor digging into her back. The blackness was fading like the coming of dawn, being replaced by another kind of silence, an eerie silence that told Sevyn the castle that was once filled with a magical energy was now abandoned. The portal was glowing, though the light was flickering and fading like leaves swaying in the breeze before a full moon. The young half-elf squinted at the light, trying to see if her spells worked. Soon, her eyes hurt from the strain and the sudden brightness, and she shook her head. Sevyn didn't know.

Slowly, she tried to stand, tried to get a better look at her surroundings, but the spells had taken their toll on her body. Sevyn settled with sitting, barely propped up on one elbow. Kaysie was laying face down on the floor, one arm curled up under her head, as if she were asleep. Sevyn briefly hoped she was, as she had sensed the human had gotten caught up in the spells, and Sevyn didn't know how they would effect someone not trained in the Arts. She tried to drag her tired, aching body to the doorway, but didn't get far. Sevyn's muscles refused, locking up in protest, her head pounding in disagreement. The mage lay back down, trying to force out the pain and grogginess. "Kaysie," she said to the body in an urgent tone,

"Kaysie."

Nothing.

"Kaysie. Wake up. It's over." This time, she was more adamant, trying to sound more confident, with a touch of boredom, like a mother fed up with a misbehaving child.

A foot moved. "Come on. We need to get going. We need to find— Quynn."

Sevyn almost forgot the name. She knew she couldn't move, but hoped Kaysie might respond to her friend's name. It worked, sort of.

"Mmmmfffffhhhhhnnnnn."

Kaysie tried to roll over, but her muscles locked up. She was used to that, riding too much, too hard. With all her resolve, Kaysie rolled over. A softly chiseled face blew soft wisps of warm air on her cheek. The soft skin, pale in the moonlight, was accented with brown eyes staring at her intently. The face appeared upsidown to Kaysie. "Sevyn," she started.

"At least you remember who I am," the half-elf said with a touch of sarcasm, trying to hide her relief.

"Where's Quynn? Where's - everyone?" Kaysie made an attempt to look around, discovering for herself the deafening silence that surrounded them.

Sevyn remained silent, then just shrugged. Something made her think of the portal once more. Maybe a flicker off of the intricately carved wood making a doorway to another plane, maybe an image of a familiar object in front of the flickering light. "In there," she said, now sounding completely confident, "Everyone is somewhere inside the portal."

"What?" Kaysie couldn't believe what she just heard. Her heart began pounding. She wished like mad that she knew all the secrets of this world that her best friend did.

"They are all in there," Sevyn repeated calmly, pointing to the portal, as if she had told Kaysie instead that there was a beautiful full moon out tonight, "But first, we need to be able to stand. The magic has taken a lot out of us. I am surprised that you are recovering so quickly, though it will still take awhile."

"How long?" Kaysie asked, her voice squeaking a bit in nervousness.

"By tomorrow we should be able to walk," Sevyn replied, slowly dragging a blanket off of her bed that she hoped would keep most of the stones from digging into her spine.

"Tomorrow?! We can't wait that long! We—uh, I don't know what's in there!" Kaysie tried to stand, but couldn't, as if her legs had given up.

Sevyn lay down on the blanket, thankful for a bit of softness. Her black hair shifted over her arm, like a long dark waterfall. She tried to use her robes as a cover. She shivered, the cold stones taking the heat from her small body. Sevyn lay there, her deep brown eyes wide open, unblinking, staring blankly at the ceiling. "You humans need sleep. Go on. Tomorrow will be long, and you will be glad you did," was the half-elf's quiet reply.

Kaysie tried to think of something to say. She was confused. Half-elves didn't need sleep? What was Sevyn doing then? She thought of voicing her question, but decided against it. Kaysie didn't feel like calling attention to the fact she wasn't from this time and knew virtually nothing. Frightened, Kaysie slowly rolled over and tried to sleep, tears stinging her eyes.

Kaysie's stomach rumbled loudly sometime later, waking her up. *I wonder how long it's been since I actually ate?* she wondered, still half asleep. She saw Sevyn stir as the human girl slowly sat up, testing her balance. "You're awake. Good," said the half-elf without very much emotion.

"I'm hungry," Kaysie said, hoping that maybe the half-elf would have something on her.

"I am not that kind of magic user. I cannot conjure up food from thin air."

Kaysie was startled a bit, surprised at the snappy answer from Sevyn. She said nothing in return, but kept her eyes on the large flat stones below her feet. She noticed drops of red on the floor, dripping like paint in a line leading out of the doorway. Blood. It was a good excuse to leave Sevyn, explore a bit, and try to remember what happened. Kaysie remembered little, save hearing Sevyn's chanting, then falling into darkness. There were voices, strange words, blackness; where were they? Where was she? Then, she woke up here, memories flooding back, and her plight hitting her over the head as if the roof had caved in around her. Kaysie almost started to cry again, but stopped herself. Kaysie wasn't sure what Sevyn's reaction would be to the tears.

Something else on the floor distracted her, as she carefully made her way out the doorway, her legs still a little stiff. Pebbles? No, arrowheads. The arrowheads that Quynn had found in the lower levels of this castle were strewn around the floor in the corner of the hallway. Kaysie could feel the half-elf's presence moving behind her as Kaysie shoved the small objects in a pouch. "Now, what's going on?" Kaysie asked, returning to Sevyn's room.

Sevyn started talking about the portal and that the others were pulled through because of the force of the magic—then, stopped. She noticed Kaysie's blank stare and decided to stop wasting her breath. She added after a short pause, "Do you want to see Quynn again or not?" It was an impatient parent-like question.

Kaysie nodded, eyes once again fixated on the stone floor. Images of Quynn danced in her head—not the ones of them here, in this strange place, but them home, with their horses, their only worry being how they might do on a test in school or in a horse show. Pulling herself together, steadying her voice, she looked Sevyn in the eye, gripped her bow, and said, "Yes. I'm ready," as confidently as she could muster.

It was darker than Kaysie thought it would be. She had it in her mind that portals went directly from one place to another, like that spell that brought her and Quynn to this strange land. Suddenly, all the courage that had built up inside the young human girl washed away like waves going back to sea. Impulsively, Kaysie grabbed Sevyn's hand. She expected the half-elf to pull away, but she didn't. Sevyn's hand was warm and little, the fingers small and thin, like holding onto the hand of a child. "Wha—what is this place?" Kaysie stammered.

"The Ethereal Plane," Sevyn said, as if Kaysie had asked what that round bright ball in the sky was.

Silence. Kaysie was glad that her blank stare wasn't visible in the pitch-blackness of this place. She heard the half-elf sigh quietly. "A road of sorts to other planes of existence. Have you never heard of other planes before? Like Heaven and The Portal City and Valhalla. We are from the Prime Material Plane—"

Before Sevyn could continue, the grip on her hand tightened. Just as the half-elf was going to impatiently ask what was wrong now, a tall thin rectangle of light appeared in front of them. "What's that?" Kaysie asked, feeling like a toddler for asking so many questions.

"A portal," Sevyn said, "Do you want to go through? It is probably where the rest of them are, as it is the first we have come across."

Kaysie nodded, then, thinking Sevyn could not see that small gesture in the darkness, she tried to say, "Yes," confidently, but she felt like a frightened mouse.

The Portal City

Sevyn was pretty sure where this portal would lead as they approached, but she wasn't sure what Kaysie's reaction to the location would be. The half-elf had always wanted to visit, so curiosity overtook her sense of Kaysie's well being as she and the young human stepped though the doorway and into an alleyway. Sevyn closed the old wooden door behind them, as now there was a small general store on the other side. Kaysie had not relaxed her tight grip on Sevyn's hand. They watched as creatures that should stay in nightmares passed alongside those with bright feathery wings and horse-like bodies. Kaysie tried not to stare, but wanted to know exactly what certain creatures were called.

Sevyn did a better job of pretending she'd been there before, not even flinching as a creature with a human's body and a purple squid-like head walked past. Kaysie thought she saw a few humans, though upon closer examination as the beings walked past, she saw more and more features that convinced her she was the only one. Small horns protruded from a creature's head that otherwise appeared human. A woman with a snake's body and six arms slithered past, glaring at Kaysie for a moment, then a creature that looked to be a yellow-skinned elf distracted the creature. The half-elven wizard suddenly took the human aside to a small outdoor cafe and bid her to sit next at a round wood table with simple chairs. "Kaysie, you need to stop this staring," she practically hissed, barely making herself heard over din of the crowd around them, "Creatures here don't judge you on appearance. It's what you think, what your beliefs are. If they

94

realize you are a Green Traveler and don't know any better, you could get hurt."

"Sorry. I am trying not to," Kaysie said quietly, then added as an excuse for misbehaving, "I'm trying to take this all in."

Kaysie shook her head as if she could not truly believe the past events she had experienced. There were a few moments of silence as thoughts whirled around her head. A low cheerful hollow voice from behind startled the two girls out of their thoughts and brought them back to reality. "You Greens need a body to show you around?"

They both froze. Kaysie saw Sevyn looking behind her, slowly, though trying to appear nonchalant. Kaysie realized as she turned that "body" was a relative term. It was a floating skull, bobbing in the air like a cork on a pond, with its mouth open, reminiscent of a smile.

straight answers from a curved one

Kaysie was not one to faint or to give into those "helpless girl"-like tendencies, but when she saw the skull floating there like it was attached to some wire from above like a bad movie effect, she wished she would just pass out. Maybe she would wake up in her own bed, this whole ordeal a strange mysterious dream. But, then, it started talking, as if it still had vocal chords. Hunter, the disembodied thing said its name was, and it claimed to be 500 years old. Kaysie briefly wondered if Quynn had encountered anything like it in her stories, then, tried not to think of her friend. The pain of the unknown made her eyes tear up and her stomach knot. She didn't want Sevyn to think any less of her; to think her vulnerable and in need of protection. Kaysie swallowed the hurt and tears and tried to have a conversation with this Hunter. He began telling the wildest of tales about the city and of planeswalking, as Hunter called this traveling between the different planes, of all the strange places he had visited and the creatures he encountered. Her head dizzied at the thought. It was all fascinating. Kaysie saw Sevyn looking straight ahead, her gaze never waning to the left or right, pretending to not be with them. Kaysie inwardly sighed. She really wanted to gain that half-elf's respect.

Kaysie looked around at her surroundings as the skull led them away from the cafe. Memories of large cities with skyscrapers reaching for the clouds back home came to mind, staring skywards at the tall buildings, gothic-like spires reaching to a featureless beige sky. "What's outside of the city?" Kaysie wondered aloud.

A hollow airy noise came out of the floating skull, like blowing over the mouth of a glass bottle. It might be laughter, Kaysie thought. "Nothing. This plane is only Kanduul, The Portal City. The only way out is through portals. And for those, like any door," he added mysteriously, "you need a key."

Before Kaysie could question the skull, Sevyn abruptly stopped in her tracks and wheeled around as if caught up in a maelstrom. Kaysie almost ran into her, but she doubted the half-elf noticed.

"Where are you taking us, wandering skull?" Sevyn's voice was bitter and accusatory, as if he had lead them like sheep to a slaughterhouse.

"Why, I am showing you around Kanduul; The Portal City; The Corridor- m'lady," Hunter answered, sounding a melodramatic ringmaster to Kaysie.

"Then, you should know," Sevyn continued, hands resting lightly on her hips, her black robes swaying in a gentle breeze, "that you are leading us directly into the Kanduul Wastelands, which, I know, is not a place for two young women nor a floating head that has not yet asked for a fee for all this sight-seeing."

Kaysie stood there with her mouth open, surprised at Sevyn's accusations. The skull stopped for a moment, the longest Hunter had gone with complete silence since meeting with the girls. If a skull can show expression without muscles and skin, this one proved to Kaysie and Sevyn that it is possible. Hunter dropped his bravado and the pompous voice and said in a low, quiet tone, "I know where all eight of your friends went. Would you like to continue now, Sevyn?" in a voice that at once implied haste and sarcasm.

Sevyn looked at Hunter, chocolate brown eyes to hollow eye sockets. Her hands clasped more firmly onto her thin hips, now mostly covered by her robe's sleeves, those cool eyes flaming. "Where are they?"

Kaysie shuddered involuntarily, then wondered if the air around them had really turned to ice or if it was her own imagination. Hunter rose a bit in the air, never taking his eye sockets off of Sevyn. "They are in the Outer Planes," he said in a normal tone, though Kaysie sensed he was still a little miffed.

"The Outer Planes are a large area. Why should I trust you?" Sevyn's voice still held contempt, but the tone had softened.

Hunter answered like he was talking to an overly inquisitive three-year-old. "Because I watched them disappear into a portal in The Wastelands. I know it goes to the Outer Planes, though I know not where. I have seen this gray-robed one before—Roustin Blackfyre, is it?"

Kaysie couldn't help herself. "Are they ok? If he harmed Quynn, I swear, I'll—"

The young girl practically had an arrow drawn and nocked in her bow, ready to go into this forbidden place she had never heard of.

"Calm down, Kaysie." Sevyn had so rarely used her name that she stopped. "We'll find them. Come on, Hunter. I hope you know the key to that portal," then glanced at Kaysie's arsenal of bow and sword and added, "for your sake."

The smell preceded The Kanduul Wastelands. Kaysie could not have prepared herself for this rancid dump of a place, littered with human scum and the abandoned trash of the city. Piles of garbage and forgotten toys dotted the landscape and lay piled in tall rotted skyscrapers. Even the ground was trash, a gross encyclopedia of the habits of the residents of Kanduul. Rats and flies swarmed over the mounds, like leeches to blood. Kaysie concentrated on not throwing up. If Sevyn noticed, she didn't react, but it was obvious that the half-elf wasn't pleased with her surroundings. The skull moved forward, barely noticing the infestations around him. Many were human, that Kaysie could tell. Others looked human at first glance, then a telltale feature gave the beings away—oddly colored hair, short, stubby horns, long razor-sharp claws. Only a few obviously had no human blood in them at all. It was these that Kaysie tried the hardest to avoid as she sidestepped trash and decaying rodents. Suddenly, one of the almost-humans cut off Kaysie's path. The thing had long scraggly dark purple hair and red eyes, like those of an albino that seemed to glow around the dark skin surrounding the orbs. Thin rags clung to its body, grimy from The Wastelands. The thing shoved its face into hers, showing two rows of jagged teeth, purple gums, and breath like a used chamber pot. Kaysie wondered why she hadn't smelled it before she could see it. Her eyes stung with the stench. "Spare a few coins?" asked an impatient alto voice that came from the creature, showing two rows of jagged teeth.

"Half-demon," Hunter muttered near Kaysie's head, "Don't trust it."

"Oh, and they should trust a floating bone box?" the thing retorted sarcastically.

Kaysie tried to back up quietly while the thing's attention was on Hunter so she wouldn't have to answer. Kaysie heard a rather nasty retort from Hunter as she backed up into something solid and moist. One of the garbage piles. Kaysie shuddered, not wanting to know what her back looked or smelled like now. The half-demon noticed her movement and turned its attention back to Kaysie as it slithered over like a snake. "Never been in The Kanduul Wastelands before, have ya, girl?"

Kaysie thought desperately for something intelligent to say. She didn't want to tell this half-demon the truth. "I own this human," Sevyn spoke up for the first time since the argument with Hunter in an obviously annoyed voice, "It is not allowed to speak unless I say so. We are in a hurry, so move!"

The command was directed toward all of them, but Sevyn shoved Kaysie forward rather rudely. Speechless, though mouthing rude comments behind their backs, the half-demon moved away a little and allowed them to pass. Hunter opened his mouth to utter a retort, but Sevyn grabbed him out of the air as if he were only a doll and shoved him under her arm sideways. "Mmfffmmnnnn!" was all Hunter could muster indignantly. Kaysie made a mental note to ask Sevyn what she meant by "owning the human." This didn't seem to be helping that "respect" issue that Kaysie wanted to address. When the creature was out of sight, Sevyn released her grip on the skull. "Now, where is this portal?" she asked, obviously annoyed at the inconvenience.

"Through there," Hunter said, miffed.

He nodded to the left where two large piles of rubbish lay partially fallen, supported by each other's weight in an oddly shaped archway. Through the archway sat an old round stone fountain. Fantastical beings sculpted long ago stood spouting putrid water from chipped sharp-toothed mouths and held long rune-etched wands that were cracked in several places. Most of the creatures were unrecognizable to Kaysie. "This," Hunter said proudly, upon reaching the fountain, "is the portal."

Olive green algae grew on top of the water, and several sprouts were visible on its surface. The water from the stone creatures splashed holes in the scum, revealing a layer of trash at the bottom and more mud-brown water. Kaysie looked at Hunter and Sevyn, then at the fountain. "No. No. Uh-uh."

"The key is a rag from one of the arched towers," Hunter said, ignoring Kaysie's adamant refusals.

Sevyn turned and tugged at a filthy red rag that was sticking out from the pile. She silently hoped that it wouldn't topple completely. The garbage stayed, the years of gunk and goo sticking the filth together. "Here we go," she said, grabbing Kaysie's hand, who obviously didn't want to go.

"Ladies first," said Hunter.

"You, too," Sevyn said, snatching the skull from the air once again without missing a beat and stepped into the water.

The air sizzled with the magical energy set into place by the portal key. Suddenly, the sights and sounds of The Wastelands vanished. Kaysie was glad of that, though she wondered briefly just what lay ahead.

swirling colors, solid castle

The place was instantly familiar, yet everything seemed out of place. Kaysie knew where she was, yet didn't—knowing, yet not knowing. The statue was right where it should be, in the middle of the grand entryway of Blackshroud Castle. But something was wrong. Something was out of place. Something wasn't right.

Hunter was still firmly tucked under Sevyn's left arm, hardly struggling anymore. He seemed to have resigned himself to a brief existence pressed against the half-elf's side. Kaysie wondered if, after all they had been through, why Hunter had led them right back where they had started? Kaysie wandered over to the window, seeing the half-elf looking intently at the statue. She was beginning to feel useless again. Suddenly, she let out a cry, almost involuntarily, like a cat getting its tail stepped upon. Sevyn sounded very annoyed when she finally spoke. "What could possibly be outside that is both—"

"—ering you..." Sevyn trailed off, seeing now exactly what was bothering Kaysie.

Instead of the trees and mountains and the stone walkways and the rest of the familiar landscape of Blackshroud, the world outside was a sea of purples, blues, blacks, and greens swirled in chaotic patterns that made bruises in an endless void. Random points of light dotting the storm like lightning gave the maelstrom its only sense of depth. "Where are we?" Kaysie felt a little frightened of the strange landscape before her and noticed her heartbeat increasing.

"This could be any number of planes," Sevyn said impatiently to her, "Astral, Ethereal, a minor elemental plane, or one Roustin created."

"One Roustin created? Can you just create a plane?" Kaysie's voice rose an octave with each word, and she was practically squeaking by the end. After a short pause, though, Kaysie realized that either Sevyn didn't hear her or was purposely ignoring her. Kaysie noticed that the half-elf was having a quiet conversation with Hunter, yet looking as if her complete attention was on the statue. Kaysie wandered silently over to the other window, intent upon hearing their words.

"You wanted me to take you to Roustin's portal," Kaysie heard the skull say, "Here you are. I know nothing else."

"I have a mace that says you know exactly where you are," Sevyn countered.

"You're bluffing," Hunter said, not sounding like he had convinced himself of that fact.

"You want to find out?"

"Uh- um, uh-uh; It is Roustin's creation. It's been here for decades. Now, will you let me go?" Hunter sounded desperate and annoyed all at the same time.

Kaysie heard a lull in the conversation and pretended to be fascinated with the colors outside. If that really was an "outside." Instead, she tried to comprehend all she had heard. A portal that Roustin had created... He had made physical space, existing outside anywhere else. What did that mean? Were there other creatures here, too? Kaysie felt very alone. She wished Quynn were here to explain all this to her. Kaysie also wondered if Sevyn really did have a mace, and if she did, would the half-elf use it on Hunter? Kaysie remembered that Jaide had mentioned that the magic had changed her little sister. Kaysie suddenly didn't feel very safe.

Kaysie felt like she was trapped in a horror movie. She grimly hoped that some giant monster intent on having her for a snack hadn't positioned itself on the other side of the door. "Well, they have to be here, somewhere," Kaysie said, loud enough for her companions to hear, but directing her words at the window.

"Mmmm," was Sevyn's vague reply.

"Shouldn't we be looking for them?" Kaysie asked a bit too tentatively.

"This statue," said the half-elf, ignoring Kaysie's question, "What is different about it?"

"Um- I, uh, I have never really looked at it before," Kaysie stammered, examining at the stone archmage for the first time.

That was when she noticed what was wrong with it. The large amulet around the stone man's neck was glowing, pulsating like an inner fire burned within. "That's wrong," Kaysie pointed to the necklace, disbelief in her voice at what she was actually seeing.

"Do you know the history of Dargontus?" Sevyn pressed, but didn't wait for an answer from the stammering human girl, "This archmage discovered a magical way to live forever. He may have achieved immortality. He put his life force in an amulet around his neck as the first part of his experiment. No one knows what happened next."

"Is this him?" Kaysie didn't feel like facing an archmage today, not when she was this close to him.

Sevyn sighed and shook her head in frustration. "No. This is a statue of him. I saw it carved when I was a child. No, human. This is Roustin," she said, pointing to the amulet.

Suddenly, a few peculiarities came together for Kaysie, but many more questions raised their hands like school children confused by the day's lesson. She began with what she hoped was the easiest to answer. "So, how do we stop him?"

"Theoretically?" Sevyn asked, looking up at the human girl, "Break that amulet."

"Is his body unstoppable?"

The half-elf again looked up from the statue to look at the girl, this time, with a look of minor impatience. "You cannot kill one who is already dead."

"Well, how do we break the amulet?" Kaysie pressed on, though she did notice that Sevyn was losing patience with her.

Sevyn sighed loudly as Hunter looked back and forth at them as if they were playing tennis. "This stone is under a lot of highly sophisticated spells. I will have to learn more about it. Anything else?"

"Yes. About owning me back in Kanduul's Wastelands. What was that?" Sevyn's annoyance was beginning to be contagious as Kaysie's voice now sounded impatient.

Sevyn closed her eyes and sighed again. When she opened them, the half-elf didn't look any calmer. "That was me trying to save your hide from that half-demon," she said quietly, "It is not uncommon for elves to own humans, as many see themselves as better."

Kaysie went silent. She felt very awkward as Sevyn went back to examining the stone mage. *I had gained the mage's respect,* she thought, *now, I just lost it.* "I can search the rest of the castle. Maybe I can find the others," Kaysie said, hoping she sounded helpful and not like a bored child to the half-elf.

"That is a great idea. Take this skull with you." Sevyn said "skull" like Kaysie would have said "manure."

"Come on, Hunter," she said, before he had a chance to protest, "Let's go exploring."

the familiar castle—kind of

Kaysie pushed along the floating skull to the far left door. "Quit shoving! I am perfectly capable of moving myself," Hunter said.

"Don't get your undies in a bunch," Kaysie muttered.

She opened the door and made sure Hunter went through. There was no sign of her companions or her best friend in this gathering area. Kaysie wondered if she should check for hidden rooms, like Quynn had been talking about back in The Dungeons. Hunter looked at her expectantly, waiting for her to do something. "Well?" he finally said.

"Well, they're not here, but are there any secret rooms, like if we pulled a book out or moved a rug?"

Hunter floated around in a tight circle with his eye sockets looking up at the ceiling. "You've heard too many stories, m'lady," he said.

Kaysie didn't say anything. She walked to the next door, a thick wooden door that would lead to the main hallway. Silently, they looked in every room on the first floor of the castle. An eerie silence filled the gray stone walls and gave Kaysie a bad feeling that she didn't remember having while back in the real Blackshroud Castle. Hunter looked around at the enormity of the rooms and the lavishness of the furniture and trinkets, seemingly amazed. Whatever was bothering Kaysie didn't seem to be affecting the skull. She wanted to question him, but decided that it probably wasn't a good idea to announce vulnerability to someone she barely knew. Kaysie thought briefly about going back in The Dungeons, but immediately, the thought of entering the dark rooms with a floating skull struck her as hilarious. She thought of a horror movie survival guide that Quynn had given her a few months ago. Kaysie made a mental note to add this one if she ever got home. Kaysie couldn't help but smile. She needed that.

The second floor yielded none of her friends, either, and Kaysie was beginning to get nervous again, though much of the castle had yet to be explored. She half expected to hear noises coming from the third and final floor in this section of the castle, but heard nothing. Kaysie was immensely curious as to what Sevyn's room would have inside. As they made their way to that second door on the right, Kaysie thought she heard a noise. So did Hunter, for he stopped at Kaysie's left shoulder, and the two exchanged a glance. Kaysie drew her short sword. It was awkward in her hands, as she was unused to wielding such a weapon. Thankful for her weight classes at the gym, she tried swinging it a bit to figure out the weight before opening the door. The door flew open and hit the opposite wall with a loud thud that echoed throughout the room as the door bounced back a few inches with the force. No one was there, though the two companions still heard the noise. It sounded like moaning; or Quynn in the morning, Kaysie thought. They went inside the large room that on another plane was Sevyn's. Two images competed for their attention, like two slides trying to overlap. One was of the bedroom that the girls had first seen, with the large bed in the far corner and the desk at the window with a large open book taking up the entire flat surface. A trunk faded in and out of clarity in front of the overstuffed bed, and bookshelves filled with magical books and trinkets fizzled on the wall. The portal, still glowing and swirling with sickly color seemed to exist right in the middle of the bed, not pausing for the several laws of physics it was defying. Larger shelves with thick tomes and loose paper ran through the desk. It was giving Kaysie a headache. "Illusion," Hunter said calmly, "One of these images is an illusion."

Sighing, Kaysie turned around, figuring that this wasn't helping them find her friends, when she once again heard the moaning. Hunter sputtered, "Um, Kaysie? Who's that?"

Confused and a bit frightened, Kaysie looked over to Hunter. "Where?"

"Down there."

Laying face down on the floor was a man dressed in leathers with a familiar mess of dark hair showing over a brown cloak. "Rilee!" Kaysie almost shouted, but controlled the volume of her voice.

Kaysie bent over Rilee's body, consumed at once with sympathy and relief at finding her friend. "Are you ok?" she asked, then thought sarcastically, that was a really smart question, Kays'…good for you; always thinking of the perfect thing to say.

"Kaysie? Is that you?"

She couldn't believe the obviousness of the conversation. She almost laughed again. "Yes, Rilee, what happened to you? I am so glad to see you!"

He moaned again, rolled over, and smiled. "I'm glad to see you, too, Kaysie. I saw Roustin, and one of his spells went off. A modified lightning touch, if I recall correctly. It's a wonder I'm not dead. I remember nothing after that. Are you ok? Where are the others? What's that?"

"Harumph," Hunter muttered.

It took a moment for Kaysie to realize what "that" was. "Rilee? This is Hunter, a friend. Hunter, Rilee," Kaysie said, looking from one to the other of them.

"Pleased to meet your acquaintance," Hunter said, reverting back to his flowery speech.

Rilee stared for a moment, then slowly stood. "Where did everyone go?"

"I don't know," Kaysie said helplessly, looking at the cobblestones beneath her feet, "Hunter and I have been looking all over Blackshroud."

"Thank you," Hunter said to Kaysie, "Finally I get some recognition."

"We haven't been in the towers yet, though."

"Well, I'll help you. And you can put your sword away now," Rilee smiled.

Kaysie sheathed her weapon, and the three of them made their way to the stairs leading to the towers.

There was one problem with that idea, however, that Kaysie hadn't known. When they reached the top of the stairs, Kaysie thought that the tower would open up at the end, like a long hallway to another part of a building. Instead, the door they reached was a thick wooden one filled with faces in agony carved very realistically into the dark wood. "This leads outside, doesn't it." Hunter wasn't questioning the girl. It was a statement.

Kaysie's heart sank. She put her ear as near to the door as her nerves would allow and heard the familiar eerie wailing of whatever it was that was out there. "Yes," she sighed, turning abruptly and leaned dejectedly against the wall of the short hallway.

Rilee looked confused. "What's outside?"

Hunter quietly led him back down the stairs and disappeared into a room with the young man. They came back a few minutes later, both looking dejected.

Rilee

The companions were silent, each lost in their own thoughts of the past few days and weeks, standing defeated in the hallway. "There is something about this place that makes me uneasy," Kaysie finally said, feeling safer in Rilee's presence.

"Well, it is Roustin's creation," Hunter said dully.

"I know that," Kaysie said impatiently, "The castle on the—Prime Material Plane, is it?—didn't make me this nervous. Something here isn't right."

"I didn't know that this plane is Roustin's creation," Rilee spoke up.

Hunter and Kaysie took turns interrupting each other, filling in the young warrior of their travels through Kanduul and through the fountain portal. "Where's Sevyn?" Rilee finally asked.

"Still downstairs examining the Dargontus statue," Kaysie sighed, "while we're stuck here at this dead end."

"Why don't we check the lower level?" Rilee suggested.

The girl smiled and allowed herself a short laugh. "Quynn and I were calling it The Dungeons."

"Well, let's check these Dungeons," Rilee smiled.

Kaysie figured it was safer and not quite as funny with Rilee in the group as the three friends made their way back down the stairs and through the hallway towards "The Dungeons." At the door to the grand entryway, Kaysie paused. They had been gone for awhile. "We should tell Sevyn where we're going."

Rilee tried to talk her out of it. "She knows that we are exploring

Blackshroud Castle. She is busy. Let's leave her to her studies."

Kaysie hesitated, remembering the impatience of the half-elf at her questioning and wondering if another interruption would further annoy Sevyn. "I think I should at least see how she's coming along. Maybe she's found something."

"No," Rilee insisted, "I really don't think you should bother her."

"But—" Kaysie stammered, "What's wrong with you? What are you doing?"

The short sword at his waist suddenly glistened in the eerie light. Rilee held the leather grip firmly in his left hand, the sudden movement interrupting Kaysie's questions. "I really don't think you should bother Sevyn," Rilee repeated, staring angrily at the young girl.

Kaysie took a step back, surprised and a bit scared. Hunter flew to her side and whispered, "I don't know this Rilee too well, but I'd draw a weapon if I were you, preferably that short sword."

Like coming out of a trance, Kaysie shook herself and unsheathed her sword. She tried to hold it like she'd used one before. "Rilee, what's wrong with you? Why don't you want me talking to Sevyn?"

Rilee advanced in two large strides. Kaysie didn't know what to expect. She lifted the sword in front of her face, the weapon still awkward in her hands. Kaysie silently thanked herself again for all her weight training back home as she parried an attack from her friend. "Stop this!" she screamed, wondering what could have come over her friend.

Rilee ignored her and came again with the piercing weapon. She managed to block a shot to her stomach and pushed him off balance with her blade. Hunter saw his chance. Quickly, the skull flew towards the man's chest, head down like a battering ram. He hit Rilee square in the stomach, the warrior grunted as the breath escaped his lungs. "Dammit!" Hunter swore, "You were supposed to fall!"

"Close enough!" Kaysie answered.

Rilee's grip on the weapon had loosened a bit when he doubled over, and Kaysie noticed. The young girl took aim like a baseball player and knocked the sword from his grasp as if she were about to hit a home run. The weapon clattered against the stone floor, skidding just out of Rilee's reach. It was then that the door to the grand entryway opened with a decisive thud that echoed in the hallway. "What in the name of all the gods is going on here?" Sevyn's familiar voice demanded impatiently.

Rilee was still doubled over, still surprised at having lost his weapon, and still eyeing Kaysie as if she were the devil herself. Hunter was floating around Rilee, not letting him move to retrieve his sword. Sevyn looked at all of them in turn, obviously angry. "Rilee, what are you doing?"

"I told Kaysie not to bother you while you were busy studying the statue. She knew what happened before," Rilee stopped suddenly, knowing he let something slip.

"Oh really?" Sevyn said slowly and in an accusatory voice, "And what was that, pray tell?"

Rilee stood silent, the faint breathing and wailing from outside the only sounds entering the castle. "Restrain him," Sevyn commanded through clenched teeth.

"How?" Kaysie implored, beginning to advance on her friend, sword still in hand.

Kaysie's movement distracted Rilee from Sevyn just long enough for her to say, "Like this," and came upon the man like lightning. With a single touch, Rilee's body hit the ground in an unceremonious heap for the second time that day. "That should keep him out for awhile," Sevyn said.

Kaysie allowed all her emotions to resurface. "What did you do to him? Why did Rilee do that? He's never tried to hurt me before."

"He will be asleep for awhile. That is all. And that was Roustin," Sevyn said matter-of-factly, "in Rilee's body. I had just discovered that the life force in that amulet is not Roustin's. It's Rilee's."

Kaysie was beyond being surprised by the events going on around her. Somehow, Roustin invading Rilee's body didn't faze her much, except for the intense indignation at the necromancer taking over her friend's body and imprisoning his soul in a gemstone. "That was a start," Sevyn was saying, "I have some rope here to tie him up with. I have no way of knowing how long that spell will last, and I cannot waste my time with him. How are you with knots?"

"I can do it," Kaysie said simply, silently thanking Quynn for making her learn to hog tie as she tied Rilee's hands to his feet, her heart sinking at the thought of her friend not truly being here. "He won't go anywhere."

"Good. Now, we need to find the bodies."

Kaysie almost choked. "Bodies?" she asked, looking at Sevyn as if she had grown a squid head like those beings back in Kanduul.

"If Roustin is using the spells I think he is," Sevyn explained, ignoring Kaysie's tone of voice, "everyone's body must be around here somewhere, the soul removed."

Kaysie looked at the half-elf blankly, for what seemed the millionth time, then sighed. "Okay... We looked in this main building, but not in the towers or in The Dungeons—er, basement."

"Did Roustin explicitly turn you away from the towers?" Sevyn asked severely.

"Um, no," Kaysie answered quietly, "We all figured that we couldn't go outside, and that's the only way to the towers."

"So he let you two talk yourselves out of it. I see. There is no problem with going outside," Sevyn said, like she was telling a child that there were no monsters in the closet.

"Then, let's go," Hunter spoke up, impatiently bobbing in the air like a cork on an angry river.

Wordlessly, Sevyn led the group back up the stairs to the door carved with agonized faces. "Duck," she said, and opened the door.

"I thought you said it was safe out there," Kaysie said, though not ignoring Sevyn's command.

"The door isn't safe," the half-elf stated, as an arrow came flying overhead and stuck in the opposite wall.

Cool air washed over the group as the door opened fully to reveal the stone walkway. The points of light grew closer as they made their way outside. Kaysie looked at them and wished she hadn't. The points of light became decomposing faces, then bodies wrapped in rags with bits of flesh floating in the breeze. Long dirt encrusted nails loomed forth from bony hands, and hideous mouths opened to reveal decaying teeth and rotted flesh inside. "Quickly," Sevyn commanded, "This way."

With that, the half-elf glided quickly to the left toward a door with faces carved into it almost as hideous as those coming towards them. Sevyn did not have to ask Hunter or Kaysie twice. With the moaning and creaking of the undead drawing nearer, the three made their way to the door as quickly as they could and slammed out the terrors behind them.

the battle of spells

An eerie silence met the group as the intense wailing was shut out behind them. Kaysie noticed that a large empire canopy bed was sitting under piles of gray drapery on a dais, a large staircase leading up and down at a curve, as if the square tower was really round. "Upstairs is Roustin's lab. I believe the answers should begin there," Sevyn said to the stairs as she started climbing.

Hunter floated as fast as he could behind the human and half-elf. If I were still human, he thought, I'd be out of breath following these girls by now. Rounding the corner, Kaysie and Hunter found themselves in Roustin's laboratory. A large wooden table's bulk left little room for the bookshelves that lined the wall or the fireplace that interrupted it on the far wall or the chairs and small table that sat in front of the cold embers. "This isn't his main lab," Sevyn said, eyeing the two like hawks, "See if you can find anything, but be careful what you touch. Do not underestimate Roustin's power or his paranoia."

Before they could go further, however, Hunter shouted, "Behind the table! Come quick! And, preferably, with a magical weapon."

Sevyn and Kaysie ran over to the fireplace, where Hunter was impatiently floating. There was a body laying the floor like a discarded rag doll. It was wearing a black robe with arcane runes stitched into the fabric with silver threads. Sevyn kicked it over onto its back. "Roustin," Kaysie said, startling like it would suddenly spring up and try and kill her.

"Yes. It is odd that he would keep his body out in the open like this," Sevyn said, mostly to herself, a very ornate long-bladed dagger suddenly appearing in her hand.

She stood over the body, prepared to strike like an angered cobra. "I'll find my parents without you, bastard," she spat, and lunged at the still body of the wizard, dagger blazing in the eerie light of the plane.

Kaysie and Hunter made no move to stop the half-elf's vengeance. Just before the blade pierced the skin of the aged wizard's body, there came a sound that stopped the hand of Sevyn and sent chills up and down Kaysie's spine. It started low and rose in cadence until the sound filled the room with an otherworldly laughter from the belly of something that had been long dead. Kaysie drew her blade. Sevyn started to continue her action, but suddenly, Rilee appeared where Roustin's body lay. "Do you think me that stupid?" It was Roustin's voice that came from Rilee's body, grinning evilly at the half-elf, "Do you think I would just leave my body where you would find it?"

Sevyn tried again to stab at the figure, intent on killing the mage. "Ah-ah-ah-h!" the voice said mockingly, shaking a finger back and forth, "Do you really want to kill Rilee?"

Sevyn stood, dagger still poised to strike. Roustin in Rilee's body arose, the illusion of Roustin's body still on the floor underneath. The half-elf paused. It was a mistake. The puppet body raised his hands as a short bolt of energy sprung forth. Sevyn fell flat on the ground, narrowly escaping the bolt that hissed as it hit the shelf behind her. Kaysie tried to overcome her fear for Rilee's life. She drew out her bow and arrow quickly and fired at the being inside Rilee's body. The arrow wavered in the air, but managed to strike his outstretched arm. He shrieked in pain and surprise. The mage was not used to paying attention to such things. It gave Sevyn time to return with a spell of her own. A long sticky mass appeared suddenly at the mage's feet, quickly enveloping his legs, chest, and arms in its thick strands. She stood, proud of herself. Kaysie barely had enough time to comprehend the short magical battle that just took place before Sevyn flew to the now prone body. "If you value your life, Roustin, tell me what you did with them, or I'll set you alight," she hissed.

Sevyn played with a growing flame in her hand like a bored child fingers a palm-sized ball. Kaysie wondered that it did not burn the younger mage's fingers as she watched the drama unfold with horror. "Ha-ha!" Hunter laughed, floating over to the stuck wizard, "No more riddles, mage! Now you have to tell me how to be rid of this curse!"

Kaysie's mouth dropped. She was certain that Hunter knew more than he ever let on, but what was this? "Come, Sevyn. Put away your toys," he said patronizingly.

Sevyn moved her hand near Roustin's face so he felt the heat of the flame. "This is no toy. Answer me."

"You would find this Rilee in an awful state if you did," Roustin's voice came back, eyeing the flame.

Kaysie inhaled, her heart constricting at the thought of Rilee not making it out of this alive. Sevyn flicked a spark from her fingers onto the thick webbing. The flame smoldered, but did not flare and engulf the body. "I'll put that out if you start talking."

Kaysie knew she did not want to see Rilee burn to death, even if it was Roustin's soul inside. She closed her eyes for a moment, but heard only silence, and she tentatively opened her eyes. The mage had broken free of the web, but how? Kaysie was beginning to notice that spells needed certain materials and hand gestures to work, but Roustin had neither these material components nor the use of his hands. Sevyn did not look at all surprised. Kaysie wondered if she knew he could get out of it or was hiding her emotions. Hunter did not disguise his amazement at the mage's escape. "What?!" he screeched, "How?!"

Roustin laughed again, the same laugh that had filled the room earlier.

"Kaysie! Hunter! Leave! Now!" Sevyn commanded the two forcefully, as a ball of flame erupted from her hands.

Kaysie didn't see what happened after that. She and Hunter ran up the stairs, not wanting to get in the middle of this powerful magical battle. Kaysie held back tears as she thought of the old kind Rilee. She allowed the thoughts to fade as they entered a sparsely furnished room with only a small high wooden table near the back of the room and a few bookshelves taking up the back wall. A small corner of the room was taken up with what seemed to be a large square closet. The door was firmly shut. "Locked," Kaysie sighed.

"I tell you how to open that," Hunter said, as the sounds of battle escalated from down below.

Frightened, Kaysie took a deep breath. It would help take her mind off of Rilee. "Ok. How?"

Hunter found some thin metal tools and showed Kaysie how to trigger the locking mechanism in the knob to unlock the door. "Wait!" he said, part of the way through his explanation, "It's trapped. I hear something—HIT THE GROUND!" Hunter suddenly shouted as a half moon-shaped blade on a long pole dropped down from the ceiling and began to swing back and forth like a pendulum.

Kaysie felt the air moving above her back as the axe finally slowed. Her heart felt like it would pound straight through her chest, though she could barely hear it over the battle of the wizards. "Ok," Hunter sighed, "Try again."

Soon, the door latch clicked, and the knob turned. It was dark inside the square room, so Kaysie grabbed a torch that had been shoved in a sconce on the wall nearby. "What's in there?" Hunter asked, hoping for some nice treasure.

Kaysie was silent. "What's there, I asked," Hunter said, a bit louder, thinking maybe Kaysie couldn't hear him over the magical battle that was being waged below.

Kaysie just pointed. Inside on two stone slabs being held up by two thick stone pillars were two people, a man and a woman, laying on their backs, who looked to be asleep. The dim light of the torch obscured details of the two, but Kaysie knew immediately who they had stumbled across. "It's Sevyn's parents," Kaysie said quietly, "It must be."

Kaysie walked inside the room, amazed at their discovery. The room had no adornments, save for the two slabs in the center. The couple lay on their backs, eyes closed, arms at their sides, a blank expression on their faces as if they were deep in slumber. Kaysie startled as she looked at Hailea Moonshade. "The woman who touched me during the spells back in the real castle," she murmured, images coming back to her through the blackness of time.

Hailea had a striking resemblance to Sevyn. The woman's long thick dark hair lay in disarray around her pale face. Though human, Sevyn's mother could have passed for half-elven, as Kaysie noticed her high cheek bones and almond-shaped slanted eyes. The elf beside her was small and thin. His angular features ended in smooth, pointed ears and long light brown hair flowed around his head. Kaysie remembered Roan and closed her eyes for a moment, thinking how much Doreann Moonshade looked like his son.

"Sevyn said their souls were kept in gemstones," Kaysie whispered, like the stones around her would tell Roustin what she discovered, "But where would they be?"

Hunter was silent for a moment, looking at the walls around him as the sounds of Sevyn and Roustin grew louder as he wondered if the stones would collapse around them. He sighed. "Well, Rilee's soul was in the archmage's amulet. Let's search this room for hidden compartments. If nothing is here, maybe he put them with Rilee's."

Kaysie shrugged. They pressed and knocked against the stone walls for about fifteen minutes with no luck, when the sounds of battle suddenly ceased. The silence was deafening after the shuddering of the keep and the small explosions down below. Hunter and Kaysie looked at each other, frozen in their spots by the walls, wondering what would happen next. They watched, speechless, as Sevyn flew up the stairs and into the room. The half-elf glided over to the two of them and said urgently, "What's in there? That room didn't exist in Blackshroud on the Prime Material Plane."

"Your parents," Kaysie said simply.

"What?" Sevyn screamed and dove like an eagle after prey into the small stone room.

Silence emanated from inside. Kaysie looked awkwardly at the skull, wondering if she should leave Sevyn alone. Suddenly, Kaysie heard a sound she thought Satan would ask her for long johns before she ever heard. It was the whispering sound of sobbing! Hunter looked at Kaysie, his jaw slightly open. Kaysie's conscience wrestled with her, trying to decide whether to comfort the half-elf or leave her alone. Before she had adequately decided, Kaysie found herself walking toward the door to the small room. The little half-elf had fallen on her knees beside the stone tables, hands covering her face. Kaysie immediately got the image of a small child, not of the powerful mage that was before her. Instinctively, Kaysie put her arms around Sevyn and whispered, "It will be ok. We'll find—uh, the rest of your parents. Really."

The human could feel the half-elf cringe at her touch, but she didn't pull away. The little half-elf only nodded, stood, and began to walk towards the door. As long as she had been with Sevyn, Kaysie hadn't noticed how tiny she was. The mage barely reached the height of Kaysie's shoulder, and she knew she wasn't that tall. She saw that Sevyn's face was red and her eyes brimmed with tears when they came out of the small room and into the large one. Hunter bobbed awkwardly, moving back and forth as if in a windstorm, though looking at the small half-elf with concern. "Um, you want to check the statue now?"

"Yes." Sevyn's voice sounded sure and clear.

As they made their way downstairs, Kaysie began to notice the effects of the battle on Sevyn. She moved stiffly, as if plagued by arthritis, and her body shook with every step. Kaysie saw that some of the edges of her robes were singed, though it was very hard to tell on the black cloth. She briefly wondered what happened to Rilee's body and Roustin's soul, then discovered at least part of the answer. Kaysie stopped on the stairs as his body came into view. Hunter must have been staring too, because he floated right into the middle of Kaysie's shoulder blades, but she hardly noticed. A tangled mass of cloth and blood lay on heaped on the cold stone floor, hair in disarray above a hood. Kaysie couldn't see the face, but she didn't need to. Tears stung her eyes as she tried to blink them away. She felt a small hand squeeze her shoulder lightly, but Kaysie didn't acknowledge it. "We'll find, um, the rest of him," Sevyn said quietly, "Really."

Dargontus

Sevyn showed Hunter and Kaysie the hollow sound that resonated from the base of the statue. "I cannot figure out where to open it," she sighed, her breath catching like someone trying not to cry.

Hunter started to say something, but Kaysie interrupted him, blinking her eyes rapidly, trying not to dissolve into tears. "Hunter knows how to pick locks. I'm sure he can find it."

Kaysie looked expectantly at the floating skull. "I can try," he sighed.

Watching a skull try and find this hidden compartment was enough to make Kaysie's tears evaporate. Hunter tapped his forehead against the stone and turned this way and that, trying to hear sounds only he could comprehend. It was enough to make her smile. Sevyn swayed a little, as she stood next to Kaysie, hands clasped in front of her. The human girl was sure the half-elf would fall from whatever spells were tossed back and forth if she did not do something. She remembered all too well the feeling she had after being caught in Sevyn's spells that created the portal. Kaysie mustered up all her motherly instincts as she tried not to smile at Hunter's methods. "Look. Sit down. You need to rest if we're going to do this." Her voice failed her, as Kaysie thought she sounded more like a little girl than a mother.

To her obvious surprise, Sevyn sat on the stone floor, unceremoniously landing on her backside, her left arm barely helping to support what little weight was on the half-elf's bones. "Are you ok?" Kaysie asked, suddenly aware that Sevyn didn't look well.

"I shall be fine," Sevyn said, her old confidence returning to her voice, "I just need to rest."

Kaysie didn't believe a word she was saying, but stayed silent. Suddenly, she heard Hunter's voice from the other side of the statue. "Over here! Kaysie! Sevyn! I found something, but I lack hands to try it!"

Kaysie gently lifted up the half-elf. Sevyn moved away from the human, walking like a toddler, unsure of each step, towards the skull. Kaysie sighed. Hunter floated near the floor, and when they came into view, he exclaimed, "I think that this stone presses downward and unlocks this stone in the base. I cannot maneuver myself to try it, though."

Kaysie knelt down and pressed on the cobblestone that Hunter pointed out, excitement building inside. It was tiny, one that would not have been noticed, that was pressed easily farther into the floor. Just like Hunter had said, a panel on the statue slid open to reveal a small circular hollow space. Looking inside, Kaysie noticed a small cloth pouch with thin strings holding it shut. It was a course material with small irregularly shaped objects inside that she locked her fingers around and pulled out of the base. Hunter hovered right next to her head. "Get back, Hunter!" Kaysie said, shooing him away like a fly, "Some of us need to breathe!"

Kaysie stood and opened the pouch. Seven small stones glowed visibly in the gray room, each a different vibrant color. Sevyn gasped. "We found them."

undead

"Now we need to find them," Hunter said, "Their bodies, I mean." Kaysie sighed. "Where haven't we looked?"

"The other tower," Sevyn said slowly, not meaning to answer the human's question, "Of course."

"How do you know?" Kaysie looked confused at the half-elf.

"There is no time for this. Just come with me," Sevyn said, a touch of urgency in her voice.

"I'm not going back out there," Kaysie said, running after the mage, "That was too close the first time."

Sevyn sighed, moving faster than her legs wanted her to, but pushed on, oblivious of the pain. "That sword of yours will work on those apparitions."

Kaysie didn't argue. When they reached the silently screaming door, Hunter and Kaysie immediately ducked, as if the same strings controlled them, as the arrow flew overhead. The howling grew closer, faster, this time, as if the undead things were expecting them. Kaysie had a sinking feeling that this wasn't going to be as easy as she drew her rune-etched dark steel blade. Kaysie let Hunter and Sevyn move past her as she tried to defend their backs. One flew like lightning toward the human. Long dirty nails reached menacingly from rags attached to a decaying face for Kaysie's head as she tried to impale the creature on her sword. It flew around her blade and bent itself almost in half to avoid it. The undead thing's mouth opened wide revealing yellow jagged teeth, and it let out a piercing scream as it flew for Kaysie's sword arm. "Now!" Hunter cried, "Run! The door's open!"

Kaysie tried to fend off the attack and run for the safety of the east tower, but felt her flesh rip as the creature sunk its teeth deep into her forearm. The floating skull pushed the creature off of Kaysie and against the low stone wall, but the damage had already been done. The three of them rushed inside and slammed the door before the undead thing could do more damage. Kaysie winced and held her arm, trying to convince herself not to scream in pain. She sat against the wall of the stone hallway, her eyes tightly closed. All she could think of was her family, her family that had no idea what had happened to their daughter, and would have no idea what was happening to her. Kaysie's thoughts drifted on mental images of her family, of Roan, of Quynn. Her eyes welled up with tears of pain and remembrance. "This should help the pain," Sevyn said calmly, pulling out some herbs from a pouch, mixing them together to make a dry poultice, and smearing the mixture on the ragged flesh.

Kaysie winced, thinking that this was much worse than when she fell off her horse and broke her leg. Sevyn then tore a strip of cloth from her robe and tied it around Kaysie's arm. "That should do until we can find you a good cleric."

"A what?" Kaysie asked, as she tried to block out the burning sensation that was beginning to slither up her arm.

"A healer. A cleric. Which gods are you fond of?" Sevyn asked shortly.

"I, ah, don't know. Nothing evil, ok?" she managed to say.

The half-elf looked at her strangely, but said nothing for a moment. Sevyn suddenly looked Kaysie in the eyes and asked, "Where exactly are you from? Don't evade my question like you have with the others."

Kaysie opened her eyes for a moment and looked into Sevyn's chocolate brown eyes. "I am from another plane or another time, I think," she said slowly, not caring anymore if anyone knew.

"That's what I thought," came Sevyn's reply, surprising the human, "You are how old?"

"Fifteen," came Kaysie's bewildered reply.

"And Carry has been at your stables for how long?"

"Fifteen years…" Kaysie said slowly, answers forming in her mind, "So Roustin… Oh, my."

Sevyn nodded. "But why did he—er, uh, she have Quynn and I find the scroll to bring us back here?" Kaysie asked.

"Roustin discovered that he could not work his magic on your plane. He knows I am more powerful than I ever showed him. Roustin stopped teaching me when he realized that I was getting too powerful, but he didn't realize that it was too late. In order to destroy me, he needed Quynn to learn magic or you to learn to be a warrior, and he realized that couldn't happen where you were," Sevyn explained.

"Why us? What's so special about us?" Kaysie winced in pain again as the burning slithered to her shoulder.

Sevyn smiled a private smile. "Both of us could sense the powers that Quynn stored deep inside, her extraordinary will bent towards magic. And your skill with the sword could be unmatched, if you had the proper training. I know of no one who could have picked up that sword and have innately known how to use it."

the others

"So, Hunter, what is this about a curse?" Kaysie asked through the haze of pain, figuring she was going to die anyway, why not learn all she could?

Sevyn looked at him expectantly. "I've been cursed to live my life like this," the skull said simply, "Roustin claimed he could reverse it. Come. We have to find the others."

With that, he floated off through a nearby open door. Before the two girls could react, they heard a cry of surprise from inside the room. Sevyn moved quickly, with Kaysie not too far behind, clutching her arm. A small woven rug covered some of the cold stones on the floor of the room, and an even smaller bed tucked in a corner covered the rest. A small figure lay on its back in the center of the bed in the same position as Sevyn's parents, looking as if it were resting peacefully. "Siriia!" Kaysie and Sevyn immediately exclaimed.

Sevyn smiled. "My theory is correct. Each of the bodies are in their rooms," Sevyn said, suddenly running out of Siriia's bedroom.

"Wait! Sevyn! Where are you going?" Kaysie called, realizing then that it hurt too much to move, as she slowly sat on the stone floor, back pressing against the wall.

"We have no time to loose!" came a reply.

"I- I can't," Kaysie tried to say to the retreating figure, but wasn't sure if her voice traveled far enough.

The noise of footsteps ceased. Kaysie thought Sevyn was gone and resigned herself to die here, on this strange plane in a vaguely familiar castle. The footsteps resumed and drew closer, this time with a greater urgency. *"Kardak tresa verdas hulvan."*

With those strange words, Sevyn put a hand on Kaysie's shoulder. The pain swayed, but didn't waver for long. Kaysie sighed, then raised an eyebrow in surprise. Suddenly, she felt much stronger! "What was that?" Kaysie asked, able to pick herself up.

Sevyn shrugged. "A little spell I picked up. It will last long enough, I hope, but not forever. Let's go."

Sevyn hurried into the next room, Kaysie walking beside the now slower half-elf. Though the room wasn't big, a canopied bed sat proudly in the far corner, several layers of silver wispy drapes hung off of the posts and thick blankets covered the mattress. Large feather pillows sat near the wooden headboard, looking as if they had never been touched. A thin figure lay on the bed, the head in between the pillows, as if the person didn't want to mess up their symmetry. The figure was dressed in a thin black robe, bony bare feet sticking out from underneath the bottom hem. Tapestries covered the walls, as if stone bothered the occupant. Vast scenes of magical battles and of long-dead mages cast their spells on the colored wool. A low bookcase crammed with books and small trinkets stood on the opposite wall. Kaysie looked at the baubles, then wished she hadn't bothered. Several skulls sat grinning up at her, holes smashed in several places. Small shapes lay suspended in yellow liquid, some with expressions of terror pasted for eternity on their tiny faces. In front of an opaque glass jar on a small wooden end table next to the bed that faintly glowed orange in the darkness floated a giant orb with one singular eye. The thing blocked the table completely and hid the torso of the body on the bed. Four more eyes turned toward the two girls on top of long dark stalks on top of the glaring orb. "By the gods," Sevyn said with a trace of fear, "An eye of death. *Faltan kirad lertana SAS'DAG dor'gam morsak reldar NIRTAN.*"

The low monotone voice of Sevyn chanting the arcane words echoed faintly off of stone. Hunter and Kaysie fell silent as a mace, faintly glowing with a yellow aura, grew from Sevyn's right hand. Concentrating on the solid image, Sevyn handed the weapon to the amazed human and went towards the jar. Kaysie stared at the most beautiful weapon she had ever seen. The handle was crafted of a hard black wood carved with ornate symbols, and the angular runes, twisting and branching like veins, glowed red as if it were alive. It ended in a rectangular mass of dark steel carved with short, wide spikes. The beaten metal reflected the light of whatever the jar contained. The eye of death hadn't moved, as if the operator of the creature was away and left his marionette dangling over the bedroom scene. At Sevyn's movement, the thing came to life, the central puke green eye focusing on the half-elf while the cat-like pupil constricted. *You don't want to be here*, uttered a simple command filling Sevyn's head. She laughed mockingly at the simple magic. *Leave.* The voice was more threatening the second time. Sevyn shook her head, feeling the magical incantation from the eye of death fizzle in her mind.

Kaysie stared at the creature in horror, the weapon shaking in her hands. Skin the pallor of a bruise covered the creature loosely, and wrinkles bunched around the giant toothed maw. Sharp pointed teeth grinned menacingly at the two as short stiff hairs bristled at their approach. Nostrils flared just below the central green eye, and eyestalks slithered in the dim light like a medusa's hair. Suddenly, the central eye glared at Sevyn, an eyestalk focusing. A light expelled from the eye sent the half-elf reeling backward from the pain, writhing on the floor and clutching her chest. Kaysie knew she was now on her own. She gathered all the courage she could muster and advanced on the large beast, mace raised. The eye of death focused another eyestalk on the advancing human girl, and Kaysie braced herself. There was a tingling sensation, like someone had run a feather over her body, then nothing. Kaysie raised the mace above her head and swung at the orb, coming down upon the eyestalk with a sickening thud. Olive green gore oozed from the jagged wound, and a horrible noise emanated from the maw. It reminded Kaysie of a cross between an angry mountain lion and a charging elephant. An eyestalk was now hanging at an uncomfortable angle, covered in the green oozing liquid. Shuddering, Kaysie aimed for the next stalk as the bruise-colored snake-like appendage focused on here, the black pupil contracting. "Blind it!" Sevyn sputtered through the haze of pain.

Her words distracted the eye of death long enough for the eye stalk to unleash its energy on the half-elf. Suddenly, Sevyn ceased to move. Kaysie's heart rose in her throat, not sure what the creature did to her friend. She smashed the glowing mace into the eye of death, making an accordion out of an eyestalk. The creature made the mountain lion/elephant noise and charged, mouth open revealing its sharp teeth and blood red gums. "Oh, no!" Kaysie said stubbornly, 'I will not be bitten again!'

Her arm throbbed as she struck the creature's central eye. The eye of death tried to snap off the hand that held the weapon, but narrowly missed, sending a stench that reminded Kaysie of wet dog and vinegar up her nostrils. Finally completely blind, the eye of death floundered for a moment before disappearing with a loud popping noise.

Kaysie immediately dropped to the ground beside the half-elf. Sevyn was laying on her back like she was resting, eyes wide open, unblinking. Kaysie saw no mark on the half-elf's body. The young human leaned over the still body, fearful of what would not be there. Letting out a sigh of relief, Kaysie felt a steady heartbeat and a slight breath on the half-elf's lips. "Sevyn?" Kaysie said, a little too loudly.

No reaction. Kaysie sighed and wondered if this was a good time to panic.

Suddenly, Sevyn stood and produced a glowing gemstone from the glass, glowing with a flickering orange like the flame that she had created. The half-elf threw the stone to the ground, and it skittered across the floor, stopping close to Kaysie's feet. "Destroy it," a low voice intoned from Sevyn's lips.

Kaysie raised the mace over her shoulder, as if she had always known how to use one. Suddenly, Sevyn's voice cried out again. "No! Don't listen to him—or me! It's—"

"Do it!" said the low voice that had first come from Sevyn's mouth.

The human suddenly knew what she needed to do. Kaysie flew around Sevyn like a figure skater on ice and brought down the glowing weapon upon the skull of the figure in the bed. The horrible sound of breaking bone mixed with the wet noise of shattered brains filled the room as blood spewed forth like a geyser, then silence reigned. Sevyn was bent over the ground on all fours, breathing as if she had run a race. The stone blinked, then ceased to glow as color seeped into the half-elf's skin. Sevyn tried to speak, but managed to only nod and smile for a moment before she got out, "Thank you for not killing me."

Hunter opened and closed his mouth, looking like if he had tear ducts, he would cry. "Now, how am I going to be rid of this curse, now that Roustin is, well, a broken melon?" the skull whined.

"There are other mages, Hunter," Kaysie said with a trace of anger.

"But necromancers! They are in short supply!" the skull continued to whine.

"What's Sevyn? Chopped liver?" Kaysie asked, slightly annoyed and slipping into familiar slang.

"Do you know how to get rid of this curse?" Hunter asked Sevyn pointedly.

"I need more time," Sevyn said, looking at the skull as if it were a cockroach, "Now, Kaysie, you need to destroy the gems by their respective bodies. That way, the soul will be drawn to them."

Kaysie only nodded as they ran back to Siriia's room. Sevyn took out a stone from the leather pouch that glowed a pale blue and held it for a moment before announcing confidently, "This one."

"O-kay-ay," Kaysie said, looking at Sevyn for signs of possession from a mage she wasn't convinced was truly dead.

She lifted the mace over her head and aimed at the blue stone. The magical mace came crashing down upon the gem, and it shattered like glass as shards skittered across the stone floor. A swirl of magic sprung forth from the shattered stone as a blue mass flew into Siriia's still body. She groaned a little, like someone woke her up from a deep sleep. Her eyes blinked in the dim light. "Sev? Is that you?"

It was a small child's voice, crying out for her mother. Sevyn went to her sister's side. "You'll be fine," she said gently, "But you need to come with us."

Sevyn took her sister's hand and helped her up. Even though

Sevyn was younger, the youngest Moonshade looked the older sister to Kaysie. Siriia slowly moved towards the door, then paused. "Kaysie, are you alright?"

"Well, no, not really," she said slowly, "One of those things outside bit me."

Kaysie looked at her wound for the first time and turned away quickly. The skin around it had turned green, and black blood slowly oozed forth. Her veins were bright red, making a web of color on Kaysie's arm. She shuddered. Siriia calmly reached over and touched the wound with the expression of a child deep in concentration. Kaysie thought maybe the little half-elf had been without a soul for too long and had lost what sense she had, when Siriia's hand began to glow. Suddenly, Kaysie's arm grew warm, the discoloration lessened, the skin closed and healed itself before her astonished eyes, and the pain disappeared. "How?" Kaysie sputtered.

Siriia put a finger to her lips to signal the girl to be silent. The young half-elf whispered a prayer of thanks to a goddess that Kaysie had never heard of. Sevyn stood silent. "You're a cleric?" Kaysie interrupted her own astonished silence after a moment.

Siriia nodded, reddening in the dim light. "The goddess Leishana allows me a little of her magic."

"There are others," Sevyn spoke up, "We need to get going."

Finding the other Moonshade siblings became easier, now that Sevyn's theory had proved correct. Jaide lay across the hall in a tiny bedroom that barely contained her bed. She lay on the tiny mattress, her right leg bent at the knee and her arm bent at the elbow. Her face reflected pain, as though she were having a nightmare or was sleeping off a night of too much ale. The torchlight reflected off the metal of a long sword with a streak of green down the center, forgotten on the bare stone floor. An old wooden chest sat at her feet, locked tightly with an intricate pad lock. A jade green stone, Kaysie thought, as Sevyn produced the gem from the bag, I should have known. Her long jet black hair stirred as the aura returned to her. The turquoise eyes fluttered open, looking wary of what shadows stood in the room with her. "Sev? Kaysie? Siriia?" Jaide asked tentatively, then exclaimed as best she could, " What's that?!"

"*That*," Hunter huffed, indignant, "is Hunter. Nice to meet you, too."

"Sorry," Jaide mumbled and rubbed her temples, "Where is everyone else?"

"Still in their rooms, we think, without their souls," Kaysie said, and explained what had happened.

"Let's get going," Jaide finally said, sheathing the sword in a dark scabbard and uneasily walking toward the door.

"Are you alright?" Kaysie tentatively asked the tall half-elf.

"Yeah, I'm fine," Jaide said absently, "Come on."

The growing group went up the stone steps, nervous as to what state the others would be in. Sevyn pointed out where the bedrooms were along the straight hallway before them, and Kaysie's heart leaped at the mention of Roan. Her feelings for him hadn't changed. Kaysie walked quickly to the end of the hall, opened the last door on the right, and went in. It was a larger room, shared by two of the siblings. Jirin lay on his back on a mattress behind the open door, eyes closed to what was around him. Roan lay in the far corner, hands clasped at his waist. Sevyn produced two stones, a rust colored round gem and one that reminded Kaysie of a large chunk of tiger eye. The two gems shattered easily under the force of the magical weapon, and the two souls flew like fiery birds to their owners. Kaysie watched Roan come back to life as if he were just waking up from a short nap, but did not rush to his side. She did not want to force herself upon him, she reasoned, looking at him shyly. Siriia did not hesitate before running to Jirin's side. "Those two couldn't be closer if they were twins," Jaide whispered to Kaysie, and they both smiled.

Roan smiled at Kaysie, and she averted her eyes and blushed. "Kaysie? Sevyn? Jaide? Siriia?" Roan blinked a few times and slowly sat up.

"Yes," Sevyn said, and began explaining the situation once again.

Siriia had a hold of her older brother by the waist as she listened to the story once again. "We still have to awaken Terryn and Breyah," she said when Sevyn was done speaking.

Terryn's room reminded Kaysie of Jaide's, but the only adornment was the mattress in the corner of the room with a twisted body heaped upon it as if thrown from the door. Kaysie noticed small carved woodland animals scattered next to the mattress in a pile of wood shavings and sawdust, a knife lying in the middle of the pile. Small dark pouches sat around the forest warrior, and dark bruises formed above them. Kaysie smashed the grass green stone with all her strength, thinking of Quynn's affection for him. The figure moaned a little, clutching at the bruises as if the pain would subside if he held them long enough. Kaysie went to his side. "What happened?" she asked, full of concern.

Terryn blinked a few times, then tried to focus on Kaysie's face. "Kaysie? Is Roustin still—"

"No," she answered simply.

"He discovered I switched his spell components for rocks," Terryn strained, rubbing an arm.

Siriia went to him and lay a hand on his arm. After a few moments, the hand glowed a soft, warm yellow. "Thank you, dear sister," he said gratefully.

Siriia only smiled shyly. "There's still Breyah," she said softly.

Discovering Breyah at the end sent Kaysie back into tears. The forest woman's beloved wolf lay in the corner of the half-elf's tiny room, an ornate long sword's blade stuck deep inside her chest. Dried blood stained the silver coat and spilled into the cracks of the stones below her still body. Kaysie turned away quickly, unable to even do Laeryna's body a service by removing the sword. When Breyah eyes slowly opened, Kaysie and the others for the first time stood silent, tears slowly falling unchecked down Kaysie's cheeks. Roan put his arm around the girl as Kaysie fell apart, soaking his tunic with her tears, emotions flailing about inside. His left arm carefully went around Kaysie in a warm embrace as he gently rubbed her back. "Shhh," the half-elf whispered, "It's ok. We're all here."

Breyah, who up until this point had been handling herself well, began to sob. She smiled through the tears at her human friend and said softly, "I always cry when someone else is crying."

Kaysie tried valiantly to get a hold of herself. Roan awkwardly let go of her, embarrassed at his actions. "Thank you," Kaysie said, voice still cracking, "That was nice."

She wanted to say that it felt nice, but Kaysie wasn't sure how that would sound. Her heart was melting, as it seemed to in Roan's presence. She also wanted to put his arm back around her, but couldn't work up the courage. Jaide looked around, worried at who she didn't see. "Where's Rilee?" She hadn't forgotten Quynn, either, but her thoughts were on the forest warrior.

Sevyn, Kaysie, and Hunter exchanged glances. Kaysie tried not to dissolve into tears again. "We haven't tried, yet," Sevyn said simply, "His is on the statue of Dargontus."

"Do we have to go back outside?" Hunter asked tentatively.

"I know a secret door to the castle," Jirin spoke up, "It's at the end of the hallway outside my room."

The large group made their way to the second floor of the east tower in silence, Kaysie walking as close to Roan as she could. He looked like a young boy just discovering girls as his face reddened in the torchlight. Jirin pressed a button that none would have noticed in the end of the hall as the stone opened to reveal a room of the second floor of the main building. "Here's your treasure room," Sevyn said to Hunter as the torchlight glinted off of large chests and full sets of silvery armor on simple wooden stands.

Hunter's jaw dropped as he flew around the room, looking at everything. He stopped near a rather large set of plate mail and said simply, "I can't do anything with any of this."

Sevyn explained to her siblings what little she knew of Hunter's curse. "You don't need a necromancer for that," Breyah spoke up, "Give me some time. I can probably do something."

Hunter lit up as if he were on fire. "If I could hug you, I would," he said, looking like he was trying to smile.

"Now, how do we get out of here?" Siriia's small voice asked.

"Over here," Jirin said, walking over to a bare wall.

As the half-elf approached, the wall slid open into the hallway. "Right this way," Jirin said with a sweep of his arms.

sparks fly

"Do you know another way into the west tower?" Sevyn asked her older brother.

Jirin shrugged. "Just the door to from the third floor at the end of the hallway."

"Well, then, draw your weapons. We have another fight just ahead," Sevyn said grimly.

As they made their way up the stairs to the arrow trapped door, Jaide questioned her youngest sister about what exactly was outside, as she drew her long word. "Undead," Sevyn said grimly.

At that single word, Roan drew the largest sword Kaysie had ever seen from a thick leather scabbard at his waist. The thick silver blade glinted in the eerie light of the colors trickling in from outside. The handle was wrapped in thin metal cord ending in a simple round green pommel stone. A twisted crosspiece wound its way partially up the blade, carved like dragon's wings. "That's beautiful," Kaysie breathed, "What kind of sword is that?"

Roan grinned, happy to explain his sword to this cute human girl. "It's called a claymore," he said proudly, displaying the weapon with two hands, "The green stone was from my great-grandparents."

"Get ready," Sevyn interrupted, as they neared the door that led outside.

Kaysie still held the magical mace. Roan readied his claymore. Sevyn opened the door as the others drew swords. The sounds of the undead screamed loudly outside the door. Kaysie tried to calm down, nervous about encountering these beings again. "Don't worry," she heard Roan say, "I'm behind you."

Smiling, Kaysie went through the door, the apparitions congregating on the walkway like they lived there. Kaysie recognized the one that tried to kill her and lunged, screaming a battle cry from deep within. Caught off guard, the creature had no time to maneuver around the glowing mace as it hit the undead thing with such force that it slammed against the stone wall and disappeared. Kaysie had no time to rejoice as another came to take its place. "We can't fight all of them!" she cried over the din of battle, "Edge towards the door!"

Slowly and carefully, Kaysie and the Moonshade siblings moved towards the garishly carved door to the west tower. Kaysie turned her back for a moment, intent on ducking behind Terryn to open the door for everyone. Suddenly, Kaysie heard a loud cry directly behind her and the sound of a sword flying through the air. She moved quickly and turned to see Roan engaged in combat with a rather large ragged undead, flesh handing from its arms, patches of dirty hair flying in the breeze, and eyes as black as the stones of the castle. Kaysie looked up in time to see long, jagged teeth fly toward Roan's exposed neck. Without thinking of the consequences, Kaysie lunged forward with the mace over her head and came down upon the back of the undead creature. There was a sickening noise of bones snapping as the spine of the thing snapped in half. Roan jumped out of the way just in time as it fell to the ground and disappeared. The group ran inside the now open door and slammed it shut with a sigh of relief. "You saved my life," Roan said, catching his breath.

Kaysie blushed in the dim light. "You're welcome."

The young half-elf took her hand in both of his and held it gently to his lips. Kaysie's knees gave way as she melted into a puddle on the floor. "Up the stairs, now," Jirin grinned at his brother as he pointed towards the stairway.

"After you, m'lady," Roan said gallantly.

Kaysie wordlessly made her way up the stairs, at once dancing inside with happiness and crying inside at the thought of seeing Rilee's body again. She knew she was not over her tears. Kaysie hung back as Sevyn and Jaide ran to the still body of Rilee. She saw the oldest sibling quickly turn away and hide her face in her hands. Terryn ran to her side and gave his shorter sister a long hug. Kaysie swallowed the lump that was forming in her throat. "There is one chance," Sevyn said awkwardly, breaking the silence.

Kaysie wondered if Sevyn felt responsible for Rilee's condition as the half-elf continued. "If someone can bring his body downstairs into the foyer where his soul is trapped inside the archmage's amulet, he may live."

"Terryn," Roan spoke up, clearing his throat, "We could probably do it. He doesn't look too heavy."

Looking at the blood on Rilee's still body, Roan took a hold of the sleeves of his loose brown tunic and with one fluid motion, pulled the shirt off. Kaysie's heart beat faster as she tried not to drool. He is ripped, she thought grinning, looking over the tanned chest and the strong arms of the half-elven warrior. Terryn decided that was a good idea as he shoved his cloth tunic around his belt. Quynn can have him, Kaysie decided, smiling at the thought of her best friend through her moistening eyes.

Carefully, Terryn and Roan unfolded Rilee's body so it lay flat. Terryn tried not to look at the giant bloodstain that covered the human's chest as he lifted Rilee by the shoulders. Jaide ran back for the stairs. Siriia hid her face in Breyah's shoulder. Jirin guided the three back toward the door to the outside, and he unsheathed his long sword. "We'll deal with the undead. You two run for the door back to the castle," he commanded.

the awakening

Roan and Terryn tried to fold Rilee's body in half as they ran
through the door, protecting it with their own. The rest of the group
came out, weapons brandished, prepared for the undead welcoming
party outside. It greeted them immediately, teeth and nails reaching
towards them. Fortunately, the undead ignored the three figures
making their way towards the door. Siriia, Sevyn, Jirin, Breyah, Jaide,
and Kaysie waved their weapons threateningly at the creatures long
enough for all of them to get back inside. There was no pause this
time. The group followed Roan and Terryn quickly to the foyer.
Gently, they placed Rilee's body on the stone floor beside the statue.
Siriia looked at Breyah. "I'm not that good," Siriia said softly, looking
worriedly at Rilee's blood soaked body.

Jaide looked at Breyah pleadingly, tears threatening to form again.
"But, I can try," she said in an unsure voice.

The forest cleric knelt down beside the mangled body and closed
her eyes. Soon, Breyah put her hand on the bloodied chest of Rilee
and began saying strange words. The room stayed perfectly silent
and still for some time before Breyah looked up at Kaysie and Sevyn.
"He needs his soul."

Kaysie looked up at the glowing amulet as tears stung her eyes.
She couldn't reach it. "Ladder?" she asked, looking up at the amulet
even her weapon could barely reach.

Roan walked over to the human girl and put his hands around her
waist. With strong arms, Roan lifted Kaysie to within striking range
of the amulet, as if letting a child reach a high shelf. She lifted the

mace above her head and came down upon the gemstone harder than she had anticipated, pent up anger and sadness overwhelming her as the shards flew from the stone setting. The fiery magic that had been imprisoned flew free into Rilee's limp body. Jaide's eyes overflowed, but she could not look away. Roan placed Kaysie gently on the ground. Everyone stared at Rilee. For a few moments, nothing happened. Then, suddenly, a moan broke the silence. Pain and memories came flooding back to Rilee as his face contorted with the sudden pain. Breyah immediately began her prayers to her goddess, hands glowing on Rilee's chest. Jaide turned and held Kaysie in a tight hug as the two freely cried. "What happened to Quynn?" Terryn asked Sevyn quietly.

Sevyn shrugged. "We have not found her yet, though Kaysie and I believe her to be in The Dungeons- uh, basement."

Terryn managed to maneuver to the door to the hallway and silently slip away, unnoticed by all but Sevyn. The half-elven man ran down the hallway to the stairs that led into the dark corridors beyond and jogged down the steps. The red glow of the magical torches lit the way to the last door at the end of the hallway, where Quynn and Kaysie had slept. Terryn opened the door, afraid of what he would discover. His heart wavered inside his chest as Terryn crept up to the bed where he could faintly see the girl he had grown fond of laying silently on her back. Her clothing was burned in several spots, showing small holes in her flesh that had been seared with the heat. Bruises dotted her exposed arms, shoulders, and face like she'd been beaten. Tears forming, Terryn gently lifted the young girl in his arms like an infant and walked back upstairs.

Silently, Terryn entered the foyer, Quynn cradled in his arms, and stood quietly. Even Rilee tried to see what was going on, then fell back down when he saw Quynn's log red hair, tears beginning to form. "One more, Kaysie," Sevyn said softly.

The human girl looked up, momentarily confused. Suddenly, her mouth opened and closed in astonishment and anger and sadness. The damage that had been done to Quynn's body was clear in the strange light that flowed through the two large windows. Kaysie found that she could not move. It was too much for her. Kaysie fell to her knees, face buried in her hands, and broke down. "I can't do this!" Kaysie cried, "I've had enough!"

Sevyn placed a rust colored gemstone on the floor near Kaysie. "One more," Sevyn repeated.

Kaysie looked at the gemstone, furious at the mage who dared do this to her best friend. She summoned up all her anger, all her rage, and screamed as the magical mace shattered the stone into millions of tiny pieces. All the courage suddenly left her again as Kaysie fell back to the floor and silently sobbed. Terryn gently lay Quynn's body on the ground as the red magic flew to its owner. Roan gently held the girl, letting Kaysie fall apart in his arms. Rilee groaned, and Breyah said another prayer for him. "Mnnnnmmmm!"

A moan of pain echoed in the grand entryway. Quynn clutched her arms and her stomach as she rolled to one side involuntarily. "Nnnmmmmmmahhhhh-ooooo," came another noise, pain seeping though her body.

Siriia ran to her side and began praying as best she knew how. Her hands glowed with a warm yellow light, but no one was really sure if it helped the human girl. Terryn knelt down beside Quynn, holding her head and stroking her forehead. "Shhh. It's ok. We're all here to help you," he whispered as he fought back tears of joy and anger.

Quynn cringed at the touch, then blinked a few times before the half-elf came into focus through the pain. "Terryn?"

"Yes."

"Siriia?" Quynn asked.

"Shh. She's trying to ease your pain," Terryn said softly.

Quynn ignored his command to be silent. "Kaysie. Is she ok?"

Terryn paused. "Yes, she's right here."

Kaysie didn't know what to do. She was ecstatic that both Rilee and her best friend were going to live, though her brain was still reeling. She tried to get a hold of herself. "Quynn!" she suddenly spoke.

"Kaysie!" Quynn said clearly.

She opened her eyes fully and saw Terryn bent over her, his defined torso leaning above her. Quynn grinned through the pain, looking up and down at Terryn's chest. "You want me to go back into a coma?"

Terryn turned the color of Quynn's hair. He didn't even bother to ask what exactly a coma was. "I'm kidding," she whispered, "You look great."

Terryn grinned and softly kissed her forehead. Kaysie noticed and truly smiled for the first time in several days. Hunter floated over to Quynn. "Nice to meet you finally. I'm Hunter."

"Geez-us! What the hell is that?" Quynn stared at Hunter, terrified.

"I am not a 'that.' I'm a 'he.'" Hunter said, slightly indignant, "And I showed Kaysie and Sevyn to this plane."

"Plane?" Quynn repeated, "What's going on?"

"Um, this is a plane that Roustin created," Terryn said, "It's Blackshroud Castle, mostly."

"Where is he? I'll get him for what he did to me!" Quynn tried to move, but Terryn gently laid her back down, the human girl wincing at his touch.

"You're staying right here, Quynn," he said softly, "He's dead."

"Dead? How?" Quynn looked around, confused.

"I killed him," Kaysie spoke up softly, "With a magical mace that Sevyn created."

tracing the runes

"What did he do to you?" Kaysie asked softly.

Quynn closed her eyes and looked down, as if recalling a painful memory. "It's over," she finally whispered, "Roustin's dead anyway."

Kaysie kept her fears tucked away that the necromancer was not truly done for. Kaysie noticed her best friend looked uncomfortable as Terryn gently held her. Instinctually, Kaysie knew something was wrong, but did not press the issue. She heard the half-elf ask whispering something to Quynn, but could not hear the conversation. She only saw her friend's reaction of closing her eyes and turning away. Terryn appeared at a loss as he looked up at the ceiling, then covered his eyes with his left hand, his right still wrapped around Quynn. Siriia looked worried, but did not speak. She continued to hold her glowing hands over Quynn's wounds. No one seemed to notice Sevyn backing up, then leaving the foyer, the magical mace in hand.

As soon as she reached the stairs, the half-elf let the tears well up in her eyes. Blinded by the bitter tears, Sevyn's heart wrenched at the thought that she could have killed Roustin earlier and didn't, fearful then that she and her siblings would never again see their parents. I shouldn't have let this happen to Quynn, she thought angrily. Sevyn opened the door to the walkway between the towers, mace raised. The young half-elf had no idea how to effectively use such a weapon, but her fierce look told the undead that greeted her otherwise. They threatened, but did not come within range. Sevyn made it safely to the door and into the west tower. Practically at a full run, Sevyn flew up the stairs and to the small room, where her parents lay. She had no soul-trapped gemstones for them. Silently, the half-elven mage walked down the narrow aisle between the stone slabs and knelt. There was so much she wanted to say to them as memories and words revolved in her head, but in the end, all she could do was quietly sob, rubbing a bruised shoulder that stayed completely covered by her thin black robes.

Sevyn stared blankly at the small pillars supporting the stone slabs. Her small body shivered involuntarily in the chill of the cold stone room. All feeling escaped Sevyn as she seemed to absorb the blank silent darkness around her. A crack in the pillar suddenly caught her eye. It was faint, as though a rat scratched at the stone, then gave up, but it drew her attention to the etchings around it. Runes carved by inexperienced hands decorated the pillar. Sevyn recognized the angular symbols immediately. A spark was lit inside her, though hope did not cross the half-elven mind. A smirk crossed over Sevyn's small face, causing her chocolate brown eyes to narrow. She carefully traced a few of the runes with her index finger, knowing from her training which ones to touch. Stone ground against stone as a panel slid open to reveal the hollow space inside the pillar.

A small wooden box carved with ancient runes and symbols sat inside on a square stone base. There was no crack denoting the top or bottom nor hinges to tell how it opened. Undaunted, Sevyn muttered a few incantations as she placed her hand on the box. A thin glowing yellow line materialized around the middle of the box, and she opened the wooden container as if hinges had appeared. Inside lay two perfect marquee cut gems the size of Sevyn's palm, both a vibrant green. She smiled again, fingering the mace beside her.

"How do we get home?" Jirin was asking, "Can we go back the way we came?"

"That would be rather difficult," Hunter spoke up, "The portals in Kanduul change according to the will of the god that watches over the plane, even if Sevyn's portal brought us there."

"We're stuck?" The half-elf looked at the skull desperately.

Hunter sighed. "Roustin had to have gotten out of here somehow. Maybe Sevyn knows."

"Where is Sevyn?" Jirin asked, looking around the room at the others.

A few shrugged, and others just looked at him blankly. Siriia leaned against the statue, exhausted from her prayers. Quynn attempted to sit up, her muscles fighting her every move. "Little One, slow down," Terryn said to her, smiling.

"Just 'cause I'm tiny." She tried to sound angry, but her smile gave her away. Quynn stopped moving, propped up by the statue, though still slouching, "I should find Sevyn," Quynn said decisively, trying again to stand.

Terryn wasn't sure whether to help her or stop her. Quynn ended up using the half-elf as a prop as she pushed off his shoulder and stood, wobbling. "Are you alright?" Terryn asked, watching.

"I feel like I got hit with that mace, quite frankly," she said, "but I have to do this, or I'll never move."

Kaysie couldn't help but laugh, remembering what it took for her best friend to get out of the house that fateful morning. "What are you laughing at?" Quynn asked, again trying to sound angry, but a smile softened her face.

"You," Kaysie said obviously.

Quynn shot her friend a look, then hobbled to the door, quiet snickering following her out the large double doors.

It was all Quynn could do to reach the stairs, let alone climb them. She took a deep breath, resolved to make her muscles obey. Quynn recalled the metal spiked meat tenderizer that her mother used on steaks. Now I know what the steak feels like, she thought. Quynn pulled herself together and made herself walk up the stairs. Fortunately, the stairs were not at a steep angle, so the strain was not what it could have been. At the second floor landing, Quynn bent over and tried to catch her breath. "You can do it-you can do it," Quynn repeated a few times before she actually believed herself.

Third floor. Quynn needed to sit. Her muscles felt like lead, throbbing at the strain. "I can't," she murmured, then, "I have to."

Getting back up again, Quynn tried to see what was in Sevyn's room. She held herself up by the doorframe and looked inside. The illusion that Hunter and Kaysie had seen earlier was still competing with the reality of what was there. Quynn blinked a few times, the images giving her a headache. She tried to make out what was really there, but could not focus through the pain. Quynn sighed. The stairs to the walkway were nearby. Hobbling, she decided to try the towers, west first, since she knew a little bit of it. Climbing the short set of stairs, Quynn began hearing wailing. "What is that?" she wondered aloud, then wished she had a weapon.

Ducking for the trap, Quynn opened the door. Right where here head would have been, another face appeared. The stench hit Quynn over the head as she saw the undead floating in front of her. This one was yellowed with age, and decaying bits were handing off the exposed flesh, ragged clothing rotting off the undead corpse. Surprised, Quynn froze. The arrow went straight into the beast, taking it down to the stone floor outside with a loud clatter. The thing squealed in pain that sent chills down Quynn's spine, but she didn't pause any longer. Gathering up all her strength, the girl ran to the door leading to the west tower and slammed the door behind her. Quynn's legs immediately knotted with the sudden movement, and her arms throbbed in pain. She noticed her bruises had changed color to a sickly dark green as she clutched her stomach and tried to catch her breath. Quynn crawled up the stairs, trying to ignore the growing pain. She heard a noise in halfway to the next floor. Was it laughter? Quynn continued slower, quieter, hoping to figure out where it was coming from. Silence. Quynn strained her ears, but still heard nothing. She tried to stand, forcing herself to move faster, upstairs, toward the noise she thought she heard. Pain is clouding my senses, Quynn thought, as she reached the landing and collapsed on a rough oatmeal colored rug on the floor. Shuffling. Footsteps. Quynn's muscles refused to move, so she made no attempt to run away or hide.

Whatever it is can kill me now, she thought, closing her eyes and laying on her side in a ball, clutching her aching body.

The sounds drew closer, then ceased. Quynn waited for a few moments in complete silence. Well, maybe it won't kill me right away, she thought, not bothering to look up. "Quynn?" a voice asked, with a touch of surprise.

Quynn recognized the voice after a few seconds. "Sevyn?" she groaned, still not moving. It hurt to talk, too, she decided.

"How did you get here?" Sevyn's tone almost implied a statement rather than a question.

"One knee in front of another," Quynn said.

Silence. Quynn was still looking at the inside of her eyelids. "Actually, I meant how did you get here, as in this plane."

Quynn was silent. "Roustin," she said shortly.

There was a loud sigh. "What happened?"

"Jaide and I tried to fight him off, but we couldn't," Quynn said, sounding annoyed.

"Did he do that to you?" Sevyn asked, her voice dropping.

"He- he used a spell," Quynn hesitated, "A strength spell."

Quynn again heard nothing from the half-elf. She shuddered involuntarily, as pain overtook her body again, stiffening her muscles. "How did you know?" Sevyn asked finally, her voice not hiding its surprise.

Quynn knew exactly how she knew. She had read too much and done too many role-playing games not to know a strength spell when she saw one, but she couldn't say that to Sevyn. "I've seen it done before," she finally said to the mage, "Back home."

Quynn tried to stand, her joints stiffening and her muscles tensing at the movement. She groaned, pain squeezing her like vices. Slowly, Quynn felt the stone under her feet, but could not continue. Out of the corner of her eye, she saw Sevyn moving her fingers in an intricate pattern and fingering something in a pouch. Suddenly, a round silvery disc about four inches thick appeared in front of the human girl, floating inches above the ground. Good ole Sordan, Quynn thought smiling, thinking of the mage who created that spell in her games.

Without hesitation, Quynn lifted herself onto the disc and tried to sit. It barely moved under her weight. "Thank you," Quynn said, her breath getting caught in her pain-wracked voice.

"That should prove easier, as it will be hard for you to go up more stairs," Sevyn said matter-of-factly.

"Up more stairs?" Quynn repeated.

"For my parents."

I wish I may, I wish I might

Sevyn clutched the stones as Quynn floated back up the stairs behind her. The enchanted mace swung loosely at Sevyn's hip as they entered the small closet of a room where Hailea and Doreann lay. "Quynn," Sevyn began as she placed the green gems by her parents, "Meet Hailea and Doreann Moonshade."

Lifting the mace awkwardly above her head, the steelhead came down twice, crashing down upon the rocks, sending shards skittering across the stone floor. Vibrant green auras came soaring out of the remains, flying like fairies back to their owners. Two sounds emanated from the two bodies, like people waking up from a long rest, and they slowly sat up. Hailea's long green dress caught the torchlight from the next room, and it seemed to reflect the aura that had just been released. "Sevraiean?" The human woman squinted in the dim light at her youngest daughter.

"I am here, mother," Sevyn said, holding back her happiness. Quynn couldn't tell if Sevyn was holding back tears, too.

Doreann looked at Quynn skeptically, seeing her as humans see in broad daylight. "Who are you, m'lady?" he asked, his voice reminding Quynn of Terryn's.

"I am Quynn, m'lord," she said, "I'm a, uh, friend."

Doreann stood and went straight for his daughter and held her in a long embrace. Quynn couldn't help it. She thought of her own family and the small chance she had of ever seeing them again, and she broke down in rivers of tears. "Sevraiean, what is wrong?"

Quynn was glad that the elf directed his question toward his daughter because she couldn't speak. "She is a long way from home," Sevyn answered simply, as her mother took her daughter from her father and clasped her arms around her tightly.

"Where are the others? Where is Roustin?" Hailea asked, looking from Quynn to Sevyn.

"Roustin is dead," Quynn choked out through her tears, "And the others are in the grand entryway."

Both looked confused. "Why there, or should I bother asking?" Hailea said in a parent-like manner.

"It's a long story," Sevyn sighed, "But we need to go into Roustin's treasure room. I have an idea on how to get us out of here."

Doreann and Hailea looked at each other, but decided to wait to ask questions. They followed their daughter as Quynn floated behind down the stairs and to the door that lead to the walkway between the towers. "There are undead out there," Sevyn said to her parents, explaining the faint wailing noises from outside, "Run."

Sevyn opened the door, her parents right behind her, Quynn floating on the disc. The horrible smell of decaying flesh hit the group as they tried to run for the door. Wailing and shrieking closed in on them fast as yellowed nails and jagged teeth sprang into view and surrounded the small group. Torn clothing floated in the breeze, and open mouths exposed more rotten flesh. They were trapped. As Sevyn reached for her mace, Quynn screamed, "Move!" and tried to dive off of the disc to shove Sevyn out of the way of an undead flying for her exposed back.

Her muscles locked up in protest, the damage too much. Quynn managed only to brush the mage's shoulder as Sevyn looked up in time to see broken, jagged teeth digging into her back. The mage screamed in pain and anger, wheeling around with her mace and sending the undead thing flying into the wall beside her. It disappeared as quickly as it had appeared. "By The Goddess! Go! Get moving!" Doreann commanded in quite a booming voice for an elf, Quynn thought.

But it got everyone moving quickly for the door, the undead trying to finish what the first had started. Doreann snatched the mace from his daughter and began swinging it with the proficiency of a master. He fended off the creatures long enough for the rest to make it back safely into the east tower.

The little mage fell to the floor, clenching and unclenching her tiny fists in pain. Quynn decided Sevyn's cloak looked like someone had taken two jagged saw blades and used them like teeth in a jaw to rip the half-elf's cloak and part of her back to shreds. Quynn immediately knelt beside her and held onto one of Sevyn's hands. "I don't know what I can do for you, but I'm here," she said, some of her pain finally subsiding.

"Feiwya, give me the powers to help Sevraiean," Doreann fell onto his knees beside his youngest daughter and lay his hands upon her wounds, oblivious of the blood that soaked through onto the ripped cloth.

Hailea stood still, hands covering her face, rocking a little back and forth as Doreann's hands began to glow with a warn yellow light. It reminded Quynn of Breyah, though the light grew stronger and brighter as the wound tried to heal itself. Still clasping Sevyn's hand in her own, Quynn felt the little half-elf squeeze back, and her tears almost began again. Sevyn has no idea how much that meant to me, Quynn thought smiling. Soon, the glow faded. Quynn motioned to the disc, still floating serenely in the air. "You need this more than I do," she said, and Doreann and Quynn gently lifted the small half-elf to the disc, still face down. "Don't move for awhile," Hailea said softly, stroking her daughter's head, "That needs to heal."

Sevyn barely nodded in acknowledgement. "The hallway by Jirin's room," Sevyn said to the wall, "There is a secret passage to Roustin's treasure room. There should he a scroll there that should help us."

Hailea, Doreann, and Quynn walked to where Sevyn commanded from the disc. Doreann searched the wall for only a few minutes before discovering the switch that opened up into the chamber. "On the left wall. There are high bookshelves," Sevyn mustered up the strength for more words, "The scrolls are on the middle shelf tucked inside the diagonal drawers."

Quynn paused, gaping at the wealth of the now dead mage. Stacks of large chests took up the far right corner, piled practically to the ceiling. Suits of plate mail, fine chain mail shirts, and all sorts of elaborate helmets lay of the floor and on simple stands. Shelves like wine racks stood against the left wall, rolled papers sticking out of every wooden diamond shape. Piles of weapons lay scattered around the room like forgotten toys. "Quynn," Sevyn said, bringing the human girl back, "You'll have to read it."

Hailea handed Quynn a rolled parchment tied with a velvet ribbon and sealed with black sealing wax and looked at her expectantly. "You're a mage?" she asked, sounding interested, "Do you specialize?"

Quynn looked at them blankly. "I-I-uh-I'm not a mage."

"You read the scroll to get you to Blackshroud. You can get us back," Sevyn said matter-of-factly, "You are a mage."

Stunned, Quynn broke the seal, untied the velvet ribbon, and unrolled the parchment. Symbols and runes she understood were inked across the page. Wordlessly, Quynn rolled up the paper then said, softly "I guess we need to be with the others."

"The secret entryway out is on the opposite wall," Sevyn said, as Doreann began searching.

Quickly, he found the opening as the wall moved outward into the hallway of Blackshroud. "Come! I cannot wait to see my children again," Hailea said, making her way down the stairs.

Quynn smiled through watery eyes and followed, Sevyn's disc not far behind. Doreann walked beside Quynn and asked, "So, where are we exactly?"

"This is a plane that Roustin created, m'lord," Quynn said, "It's Blackshroud, only there are a few differences."

Doreann smiled to himself at the properness of the human girl. "Please. Call me Doreann. Many elves have taught you to be pretty proper, haven't they?"

Quynn stifled a laugh as she thought of her games. "Yes, uh, Doreann."

"So, what are these differences?" he asked as they made their way down.

"Well, that room you and your wife were in does not exist on the Prime Material Plane, and there are some small differences on the statue in the foyer," Quynn said helpfully, "But other than that, I do not know."

Their conversation was cut short by a short cry from Hailea. One of the siblings had heard talking and had opened the door to the hallway. Suddenly, Hailea was running to the door, embracing one of her children. Quynn guessed it was Siriia by the height of the person. Quynn was right, as long blonde hair moved around the woman's body as Hailea rubbed her daughter's head. Quynn tried not to pay too much attention to the family reunion as tears began to form in her eyes. Instead, she focused on the writing on the scroll in her hands. She knew from her games how this sort of spell worked, and Quynn knew she needed to word it correctly or face unknown consequences. Mumbling, she went over the names of everyone in the room. "Siriia Moonshade, Sevyn Moonshade, Jirin Moonshade, Hailea Moonshade, Doreann Moonshade, Rilee Ravynsclaw, Kaysie Haggerty, Breyah Moonshade, Hunter, Terryn Moonshade, Roan Moonshade, Jaide Moonshade, and me. Back to the foyer of Blackshroud Castle on the Prime Material Plane, four day's ride from Keldon's Hill."

Suddenly, Quynn realized that everyone was silent and staring at her. "What?" she asked looking around.

"Um, are you just getting our family straight or did you need something?" Terryn asked grinning.

Quynn pretended to glare at the attractive half-elf. "I'm trying to get you all home!" she said, "And I can't do that without knowing everyone's full name. Just in case."

"In case what?" Kaysie looked nervous.

"The way this spell works," Quynn explained to the group, "is that it has to be worded perfectly or strange things could happen. There is a stronger spell of similar nature that would be harder to word, but I think I have this one down okay."

Kaysie didn't look convinced, but before she could voice her discontent, Quynn began the incantations, her voice rising and falling in a musical cadence. *"Gordul-belrant-jersa'd-korwil-NER-das-asranu-Oralia–eimun-jerhas-kortn-sank'r-o-ved-sertani-KORELA-Siranasea Moonshade, Sevraiean Moonshade, Ehirrjirin Moonshade, Hailea Moonshade, Doreann Moonshade, Rilee Ravynsclaw, Kaysie Haggerty, Breyanathesti Moonshade, Hunter, Terrynoust Moonshade, Roanallyn Moonshade, Systiri Moonshade, and Quynn Dornoch- Take us back to the foyer of Blackshroud Castle on the Prime Material Plane!"*

Prime Material

Quynn tried her best to picture the foyer in Blackshroud Castle, back where they were supposed to be. The air sizzled around them as everything grew suddenly black. Then, the noise stopped. Quynn didn't notice any light coming through her closed eyes and for a moment, worry overcame her, scared that the spell failed. When she finally opened them, she realized that it was evening back at Blackshroud. Quynn sighed a sigh of relief. She had done it. Quynn looked around, making sure everyone was there. There was someone missing, she felt deep inside, but could not figure out whom. "Who's not here?" Quynn asked, worried, mentally going over everyone that she had spoken in the spell.

Hailea looked around. "Sevyn, Siriia, Breyah, Terryn, Roan, Jaide, Jirin, Kaysie, Rilee, and Doreann. We're all here."

"Hunter!" Quynn exclaimed, her eyes darting around the room, "Where's Hunter?"

"Who's Hunter?" Doreann asked, confused.

"The floating skull! Where'd he go?" Quynn looked frantically around, not seeing anything floating, even the disc that Sevyn had been on.

"I'm right here," said a low amused voice that did not sound like Hunter's hollow voice at all.

Like marionettes, they all looked at once to see a tall young elven man. He had long white blond hair and sea blue eyes and stood by the main door dressed rather sharply in black and grays, a black cloak with silver runes wrapped around his solid body and a dagger at his waist. "Hunter?!" Kaysie and Quynn exclaimed in unison.

"That's what I usually go by, yes," said the elf with a bemused grin, looking at the astonished girls, "though my true elven name is Keiltsahrean, which means Hunter Elf in the human language."

It was obvious he was loving this.

"But the curse—" Kaysie stopped short.

"Was removed when we changed planes, apparently," Hunter said.

"Your stories—" Kaysie couldn't complete a sentence.

"All true!" Hunter laughed, holding up his hands. "And you can't tuck me under your arm again, Sevyn!"

Sevyn opened her mouth to say something, then seemed to decide against it. She shook her head, ignoring the pain from the deep wound she got at the hands of the undead. "You don't look 500 years old," Kaysie finally spit out, eyeing the elf.

"I'm not. I'm 115, but I was in that form for 500 years," Hunter said, then added looking down at himself, "Though it didn't seem to affect my true form."

Kaysie rolled her eyes. "Yes, that's Hunter, all right."

Quynn cleared her throat. "Um, Sevyn? About getting me and Kaysie home?"

Sevyn looked at the human girl. "That spell was the only way we could get back here, and that's the only one in existence that I know of, though you can go through all of Roustin's things, seeing as he won't be needing them."

Roan and Terryn looked at each other, dejected. Each were lost in the same river of sorrow, thinking of the day when Quynn and Kaysie would no longer be there. "We'll help you," Terryn said resolutely, putting his hand on Roan's shoulder.

"Okay," Quynn said, "Right this way, now that the walkway is safe. Sevyn?"

"Yes?"

"You, too, seeing as you know what you are looking for?"

"If you want," she said.

"I'll make something for all of us to eat," Jaide decided.

"I'll help," Rilee spoke up, smiling at Jaide.

Hunter looked at Jaide and Rilee glowing in each other's presence, then looked back at Quynn, Kaysie, Roan, Terryn, and Sevyn. "Right. To the treasure room it is!"

searching for a spell in a haystack

The six of them entered into the treasure room and sighed in unison. Hunter was actually pleased because he remembered the room as so much larger. The others knew the size and still were not pleased at the situation. "This could take days," Kaysie said sullenly.

"I do have one idea that may shorten that," Sevyn spoke up, and began to weave a spell.

She concentrated for a few moments, then looked around the room. "No," she sighed, "There are none of the same spells here as the one that was used to transport us back, though there may be those of the higher power. I cannot locate those, since I have not used one. Bring all the scrolls to this shelf," Sevyn pointed to a nearly empty scroll shelf, the wooden boards making diamonds to hold the papers, "And I shall look at them all."

"Would I be able to know what I am looking at, if I saw it?" Quynn asked.

"Yes and no," Sevyn replied, "Yes, you could understand one off of a scroll, but I would be able to decipher it without spending very much time poring over it."

Terryn led Quynn over to the far right corner, where stacks of scrolls lay in several large open chests. Roan and Kaysie strolled over to the left wall, where another scroll shelf stood built into the stone. Hunter stayed with Sevyn in the back of the room and began to go through a nearby chest filled with an odd assortment of items and papers. "I can help," Hunter said casually to Sevyn in a voice only she could have heard.

"How?" Sevyn asked absently, taking down scrolls from the shelf, looking at them briefly, and categorizing them by the spells written on the parchment.

There was some shuffling behind her, then Hunter produced a parchment. "This spell will make you fall in love with me."

That got Sevyn's attention. "What?" she whispered, trying not to draw the attention of the others and looking at the elf incredulously.

Hunter smiled and showed her the parchment. Sevyn snatched the paper and quickly scanned the page. "This produces flowers from barren ground. Why—"

Hunter took the scroll back from her and read it aloud. He bowed low and handed Sevyn a large bouquet of red roses! Sevyn looked around, seeing if the others had noticed flowers sprouting from Hunter's hands. If they had, they did not turn around. "You're a mage," Sevyn said in an accusatory tone, hands firmly on her hips, "And you couldn't have said something earlier?"

"Why, yes I am. And it would have done you no good, m'lady, seeing as I had no hands," Hunter said gallantly.

She sighed loudly and turned back to her work, laying the flowers beside her.

Kaysie was paying more attention to a suit of armor than to finding the scrolls. She fingered the smooth steel chains of a shirt on a simple wooden stand in wonderment, trying to figure out how anyone could fashion something so tiny into armor. "What do you think?" Roan asked her, putting a couple of scrolls in an empty chest beside him.

"Huh? Oh- this. It's lovely. The chain rings- they are so tiny," Kaysie said, admiring the fine workmanship.

"It's called elven chain mail," Roan smiled proudly as if he had made it himself, "It's made especially for elves."

Quiet reigned soon after, as the two of them resumed looking for scrolls. Roan turned an idea over in his head as he searched, smiled to himself, then broke the silence. "M'lady," Roan spoke up quietly, "Would you care to walk around the gardens after sunset?"

Kaysie jumped up and down, screaming inside like an over

enthusiastic two-year-old. "I'd love to," she said quietly, looking around to see if anyone else heard. No one seemed to be paying attention.

Quynn was taking her time, though she missed her home greatly. She was fascinated with the intricate drawings and the perfect script of the scrolls. The human girl began poring over one particular scroll, thinking that she might be able to learn the spell. Excited, Quynn sat on a low wooden chest as if it were a bench and began to read, fingering each letter as she went. Terryn stared at the human, mesmerized by her. He didn't think that Quynn noticed, as she was pretty absorbed in her spell. Terryn quickly turned back to the scroll shelf he was looking over, embarrassed when Quynn finally looked up. "I'm putting this down now," Quynn said as if Terryn had scolded her for not helping, though the corners of her mouth were turned slightly upward.

She stood, carefully trying to copy what the scroll asked of her. Soon, a small globe of light appeared in her hand. Startled, Quynn lost concentration, and it disappeared.

"Practicing?" Terryn asked, amused.

"I-uh-um-it…worked," Quynn stammered.

Terryn tried not to laugh too loudly. "Yes, my little mage."

Quynn blushed as red as her long hair. "I'm yours, now?" she asked a bit teasingly and a bit flirtatiously.

"If you want me," Terryn said mostly to the shelf.

Quynn slipped her left arm around his waist and sat her head on his arm.

"Sheet of flame, illusion, illusion, summoning," Sevyn mumbled, setting the papers in different piles, "Magical weapon, temporary strength—" she shuddered as she looked briefly over a scroll, silently putting the sheet of parchment on the largest pile around her, "Something I need to learn."

Hunter chuckled and picked up the scroll. Glancing over the symbols and runes, his eyes grew wide, and his face took on a pallid color. "You want to learn this?"

Sevyn shrugged, looking nonchalant as she went through more of the scrolls. "You never know when one might need a spell that turns blood to dust."

Hunter eyed the half-elven mage. "I'm not that evil," Sevyn said after a brief pause, glaring at the tall elf.

"I meant to imply nothing of the sort." Hunter's tone reminded Sevyn of his old pompous ways, but when she looked into his eyes, all the half-elf saw was hurt. "It's just a very…difficult…spell. That is all."

Hunter's voice was quieter as if he didn't want anyone else to hear. Kaysie's hesitant voice from the other side of the room broke their uncomfortable silence. "May I…uh…have—"

Sevyn didn't glance up or even pause from looking through the scrolls. Distractedly, she said, "You may have what you wish."

Kaysie's eyes grew wide with surprise and jubilation as she fingered the elven chain that she and Roan discovered fit her perfectly. Roan grinned. "Kaysie says 'thank you,' Sev,"

Sevyn mumbled a reply. She was paying more attention to the odd sensation in her head. It was as if someone were poking her brain as someone would tap another on the shoulder to get their attention. The young mage concentrated as words began to form in her thoughts. "Dinner's ready," Sevyn heard.

"It seems that Jaide and Rilee are through preparing our evening meal," she said loudly enough for her words to echo off of the stone and treasure around them with a hint of bemusement.

Quynn turned, obviously confused. "How?" she sputtered.

Sevyn smiled a private grin. "A modified spell that Rilee was working on. I didn't know he had finished." There was a short pause before she continued. "Telepathy, Quynn," she said, "Come, before the food becomes cold."

family dinner

The group managed to sit themselves around the kitchen table rather comfortably, though with little elbowroom. Jaide and Rilee concocted quite a homecoming meal of smoked venison, sliced potatoes covered in a thick cheese and thinly sliced mushroom sauce, and for dessert, Rilee's specialty, an apple pie drizzled with caramelized sugar. Pitchers filled with ice cold apple juice and goat's milk sat on the table alongside the great platters of food. Kaysie had never eaten anything so wonderful in her life, and the rest of the group seemed to agree as compliments broke the long silence of people shoving food into their awaiting mouths. "Mother and father helped, too," Jaide said modestly.

"I handed you the peeled apples," Doreann said, smiling at his oldest daughter.

Quynn tried to savor the moment of this family reunited , a family laughing and eating around the table where they had left off. She fought the tears that were springing into her eyes as Quynn thought of her own family sitting around the table without her. Beside her, Kaysie must've noticed her friend's distress, for the girl subtly put an arm around her friend for a discrete hug.

As one by one, the plates were emptied, and the food disappeared, Quynn gathered the courage to ask the question of which she already thought she knew the answer. At a pause on the conversation, Quynn asked, "Am I really in my stories? Were those tales I always just thought were fantasy…"

Quynn stopped suddenly, hearing the deafening silence that

160

followed her question, words failing her. "Let me ask you this," Sevyn said, "What were some of those supposed stories called?

"The titles?" Quynn was startled and confused by the question, but she tried to answer as best she could. "Um, *The Mage and the Amulet*, *Fight for the Heavens*, *Mists of Silverglen*, *The Passage Trilogy*, and *The Magical Tales of Ansari* are some. Why?"

The young mage ignored the astonished faces on the group around her as she made her way towards the door to the hallway. "Come," she said to Quynn, though everyone stood and followed the half-elf to the luxurious study.

Sevyn pointed to several shelves behind the overstuffed red chair that Kaysie and Quynn had both hid behind so long ago. There, inscribed in gold and silver leaf along the spines of tomes lining the shelf were the books Quynn had listed and more she had not, chronicling the history and times of the land and its people. "These are the histories of this land. Your books are all true," Sevyn said quietly.

"I knew it," Quynn said softly, "Somehow… It all makes sense."

Kaysie stood next to her best friend, aghast at what had just been uttered. "But why, then, was it remembered only as children's tales, as bedtime stories?"

Sevyn opened her mouth to answer, but Hailea interrupted her daughter. "Because humans are too skeptical for their own good. They cannot believe in magic and in creatures that are different from themselves. Slowly, it is all dismissed as myth and legend; stories to tell by a roaring fire. The magic ebbs from human veins, ignored and unused. Creatures die or find new homes as their worlds are destroyed. Faith is lost in the gods that once roamed freely alongside us in this world. All that is left are memories that fade into tales and legend."

There was a silence as the human woman's wise words sank into each one present. Kaysie shook her head, guilty of being one of those skeptical humans. She quietly vowed to be different from now on, to be more open to the fantastical. Kaysie suddenly spoke up, a though suddenly crossing her mind. "Sevyn, you made the portal to

The Portal City. Can you not, then, make a portal back to our home?"

Sevyn shook her head. "Time travel spells are not well-documented and is not something I have studied. Quynn, you would have to research such a spell. That would require much time and patience. You could become quite a mage in the meantime, though, if you wished."

Roan, Terryn, and the rest of their new friends smiled at one another. "You may stay here if you wish," Doreann spoke up, bowing low to the humans, "I'm sure Sevraiean would love an apprentice, and Hailea and I wouldn't mind two more daughters."

His wife nodded and smiled at her husband, her face glowing at Quynn and Kaysie, waiting expectantly for an answer from their youngest. For the first time since any could remember, a genuine smile crossed Sevyn's lips. "I'd be honored to help," she said, "And I am sure my father and others would be more than willing to teach Kaysie the finer points of wielding weaponry?"

"Of course!" Roan said, his eyes twinkling at Kaysie.

"You, Hunter?" Sevyn asked, the corners of her mouth still pointed upwards and light twinkling in her eyes, "Would you assist me in helping to teach Quynn?"

Hunter bowed low. "I would love to."

"You don't need to stay in The Dungeons anymore. There are plenty of rooms in the castle to choose from," Breyah spoke up, "You, too, Rilee and Hunter, if you desire."

"Thank you m'lady," Hunter said, and Rilee smiled, "We would be honored to stay with your fine family."

Kaysie yawned. "I'll pick out something when the sun rises again. I can sleep one more night in The Dungeons."

It seemed catching as Quynn mimicked Kaysie's tired yawn. "Yes. There's a lot of cleaning to do, too, what with getting rid of all of Roustin's old things." She thought of the dead creatures floating in jars in Roustin's bedroom and shuddered.

"Then, let's all get to sleep. It is late. Sleep well," Doreann said in true father form.

* * * * *

Printed in the United States
63882LVS00002B/181